Cherry Jankowski was having an erotic dream . . .

Lately, to her consternation, her dreams had gotten wilder and sexier even though she got plenty of sex every day in her job as a Joyful product tester. Her job included having sex with dildos, vibrators, animals, water massage equipment and human beings. It was hard work. And Cherry was longing for compensations in her personal life which so far had eluded her, perhaps in the way that true amusement eludes somebody who works every day in an amusement park.

Blonde, beautiful, nineteen years old, Cherry mumbled and tossed in her sleep. The early morning light falling on her face was soft and orange. A slight breeze though her opened window stirred a few wisps of blond hair on her blemish-less forehead. Her lips were slightly parted, showing a bank of perfect white teeth. She was endowed with the sensuous, pouting sort lips that old, red-nosed winos love to look at while they masturbate.

Books by John A. Russo published by
BURNING BULB PUBLISHING.

The Academy
The Awakening
The Booby Hatch
Dealey Plaza
Living Things
Limb to Limb
Night of the Living Dead

Most Burning Bulb Publishing books are available at special quantity discounts for bulk purchases for sales promotions, premiums or fund raising. Special books or book excerpts can also be created to fit specific needs.

For details, write to our marketing department at info@burningbulbpublishing.com or via standard post at Burning Bulb Publishing, P.O. Box 4721, Bridgeport, WV 26431

THE
BOOBY
HATCH

JOHN A. RUSSO

Burning Bulb
PUBLISHING

The Booby Hatch
by **John A. Russo**

Burning Bulb Publishing
P.O. Box 4721
Bridgeport, WV 26330-4721
www.BurningBulbPublishing.com

Cover illustrated by Gary Lee Vincent with elements from *The Booby Hatch* theatrical release.

First Burning Bulb Publishing printing.

Edition ISBN Paperback 978-0692256213

Printed in the United States of America

Library of Congress Control Number: 2014945776

WARNING!!!
FOR ADULTS ONLY!!!

This novel is an erotic satire, perversely intended to shock the prudish sexual sensibilities that pervaded American life and literature prior to and during the Sex Revolution of the 1970s. One of its predecessors was the novel *Candy* written by Terry Southern and daringly published to great critical and financial success by Playboy Press.

My novel was originally titled *The Liberation of Cherry Jankowski*, and like *Candy* it is intentionally way "over the top" -- as if we, at that time, needed to have all types of sex splashed all over us (pun intentional), so we could get it all out of our system and then settle down to some kind of sexual "normality." As if there really is a definite and definable normality when it comes to sex.

Not long before I wrote this novel, one could not print the word "fuck" in any book except the ones kept under the counter in the sleaziest of book stores. For example, when Norman Mailer wrote *The Naked and the Dead,* his classic novel of World War Two, his publisher forced him to come up with a substitute for the "F Word," and the word he came up with was "fug." That was the state of things way back then; we were fugging, not fucking. Mailer was one of the authors who were trying to lead the fight for candidness and real, as opposed to theoretical, freedom of speech in our literature, but it was a hard fight and he didn't always win all of the battles.

Like *Candy, The Liberation of Cherry Jankowski* was made into a movie; in fact, the movie was made first, and then I novelized it. I co-directed the movie. When it was released by Independent-International Pictures, it was re-titled *The Booby Hatch*, and edited so as to get the obligatory "R" rating. A few years ago, one of my fans suggested that it should have been called *Night of the Giving Head*. I really liked that, but someone came out with a porno of the same name, so for now, we'll stick with *The Booby Hatch*.

By the way, you can still buy the movie version of *The Booby Hatch*. But I warn you, it's not nearly so "over the top" as this novel. So if you want the real stuff, read this!

PROLOGUE

The ensuing chronicle is the true story of Cherry Jankowski and Marcello Fettucini, who were both product testers for Joyful Novelties, Inc., during its heyday. I must acknowledge a debt of gratitude here to the multitude of you who wrote letters urging me to undertake such a book, out of your fervent zeal to discover what it must have been like to be a product tester for Joyful when it was rising to become the nation's leading manufacturer of products designed to enhance the pleasures of sex and orgasm.

In a mood of flippancy and lightheartedness which echoes the zany free spirit of the product testers themselves, I have not hesitated to title this work somewhat informally – at the risk of putting off those fussy-type scholars who will no doubt come forward to protest that informality has no place in a scholarly presentation. I will defend the new title of this noble work, *The Booby Hatch*, on the grounds that it was the universally accepted nickname for Joyful Novelties, Inc., and was used unhesitatingly by all the product testers, not out of disrespect, but out of a good-natured appreciation of the pun contained in the phrase and the sentimental irony thereby connoted.

When we think of the life of a product tester, we are prone to conjure up images of having sex every day and getting paid for it, while also enjoying the inner satisfaction of being a contributor to the sexual advancement of mankind; but interesting and exciting as the work sounds, it is not always a bed of roses. Cherry Jankowski and

Marcello Fettucini both suffered a kind of psychological malaise stemming from the rigors of their strenuous daily routine on the job; at least that is what my research seems to bear out. In the interest of a smooth presentation, I could have glossed over everything and made it seem utterly splendid day in and day out, but I did not wish to insult your intelligence. My good name rests on my solid reputation for always writing the truth as nearly as it can be discerned and depicted; and besides, Joyful Novelties has had accolades enough without needing to be thought perfect. So I have revealed the company's flaws and shortcomings where they have seemed apparent in an operation otherwise noted for its pioneering, innovative spirit and its thorough organizational efficiency.

Joyful was founded in 1953 by imaginative, hard-driving entrepreneur Theophilus Suck, the first of the Sex Barons, who rose to dominate his chosen field because of his uncanny ability to get in first and score big profits where others had not even begun to sniff out a hot market. In 1953 there was no *Penthouse* magazine, nobody admitted to carnal relations with his sister, monopede mania could not be mentioned in polite circles, and most people were close-minded enough to think of you as a pervert if you masturbated by putting your penis in a warm grapefruit or a blender or a vacuum cleaner. In other words, when Suck became aroused enough to enter the sex business in a big way, it was still virgin territory. Sensing the rise and swell of the forthcoming sexual revolution long before the social scientists noticed a tingle in their collective testicles, Suck began manufacturing dildos and vibrators and today still manufactures those staples along with whips, chains, Party Dolls, simulated vaginas, artificial breasts and buttocks, and countless other erotic

2

devices guaranteed to provide "The Ultimate in Sexual Fulfillment."

Theophilus Suck was among the first to realize that Space Age technology could be applied to matters which had hitherto been regarded as private and intimate. In his firm hand, sex and orgasm became the new frontier of creative scientific innovation. Dozens of items hot off the drawing boards were developed and perfected in the Joyful Laboratories. Under the watchful eyes of dedicated Joyful scientists and engineers, male and female product testers subjected each new Joyful product to strenuous tests. Only the finest and most effective and most satisfying erotic devices were released onto the general marketplace, where insatiable public demand soon made them a familiar and indispensable ingredient of our modern, fast-paced, exciting lifestyle.

The orgasm of our great-grandparents was a weak and pitiful thing compared to the orgasm of today. The amplified orgasms made possible nowadays by judicious application of scientific and technological principles are vastly superior to the old-fashioned kind that our primitive ancestors had to reach on their own, unaided.

Thanks to the gritty determination and pioneering spirit of the men and women of Joyful Novelties, today we reach heights of sexual ecstasy undreamed of by past generations. It is my fond hope that this humble work of mine might reflect credit and admiration upon those whose diverse skills and prodigious physical prowess have brought us to where we are today.

CHAPTER 1

On a sultry summer morning, a few minutes before her alarm would go off, waking her to get ready for work at Joyful Novelties, Cherry Jankowski was having an erotic dream. Lately, to her consternation, her dreams had gotten wilder and sexier even though she got plenty of sex every day in her job as a Joyful product tester. Her job included having sex with dildos, vibrators, animals, water massage equipment and human beings. It was hard work. And Cherry was longing for compensations in her personal life which so far had eluded her, perhaps in the way that true amusement eludes somebody who works every day in an amusement park.

Blonde, beautiful, nineteen years old, Cherry mumbled and tossed in her sleep. The early morning light falling on her face was soft and orange. A slight breeze though her opened window stirred a few wisps of blond hair on her blemish-less forehead. Her lips were slightly parted, showing a bank of perfect white teeth. She was endowed with the sensuous, pouting sort lips that old, red-nosed winos love to look at while they masturbate.

Cherry's boyfriend, Herman Longfellow, watched Cherry with mixed emotions while she tossed and turned on the sweat-dampened sheets. When her hands began fondling her breasts and pinching her nipples in her subconscious throes of passion, he knew for sure she was having a lewd dream filled with wild, steamy sex, and wished wistfully that the dream could completely satisfy her, thus relieving *him* of the responsibility. He had never made love to sweet, desirable Cherry, and he did not yearn to. He was a transvestite. But his ego was gratified nonetheless when he heard Cherry moaning *his* name, rather than someone else's, in her sleep. She did not know about his transvestism; thus far in their relationship he had succeeded in keeping it from her. Though he did not desire her sexually, he did not mind being desired *by* her, and it pleased him to know that he could have her any time he wanted to, as much as it pleased him to know he would never want to. This was his secret. It enabled him to live with Cherry while she paid the rent and bought groceries, and so forth, while he devoted himself to writing a book of poems which he was certain would catapult him into literary greatness.

Herman's last name was Polsizinski, but he had it changed to Longfellow soon after he discovered his calling. He liked the idea of having a distinctive and quite literary *nom de plume;* it made him feel that he belonged securely to the world of *belles lettres*; and it also alleviated his fear that nobody would buy poems from somebody named Polsizinski. He was not airy and flighty like some poets. He wanted his stuff to *sell*. He wanted to get rich. Like Liberace and Truman Capote, he wanted to flout his eccentricities. One of his secret ambitions was to go on the *Tonight Show* dressed as a lady. If he could only get famous and rich, what the world now called strange would be called quaint and charming.

While Cherry was having her erotic dream, Herman was stretched out next to her on the queen-sized bed, reading his favorite collection of poems by Edgar Guest and titillating himself by peeping up every now and again to observe Cherry writhing feverishly and running her hands up and down her curvaceous young body. Her nipples were distended to a frightful degree, her breasts swollen into over-ripeness, while her hips moved piston-like and her thighs clenched and unclenched, squeezing delicious teasing sensation from her moistened clitoris.

Still asleep, she began calling Herman's name softly and passionately. "Herman...oh, Herman... please... Oh...*please, Herman...now...NOW!*"

Slipping her hand inside her panties, where it tingled for a moment against her *mons veneris*, Cherry soon had her fingers fluttering and working deep in the warm, wet place that was the focus of the fire that raged within her.

Torn between the desire to watch and the desire to study another of Edgar Guest's poems, Herman gave in to watching as Cherry made the bed heave so much that reading was impossible. He didn't know it, but he had appeared in her dream tremendously endowed, with a penis the size of a fire hydrant. She was staked out on the ground, a sex slave to a tribe of naked Apaches. Her legs spread wide and tied down with leather thongs, she heaved and tossed her hips and loins with hungry abandon. But suddenly there were no Indians present. Instead there was Herman with his gigantic penis, like a character drawn by Aubrey Beardsley, and he pranced and pirouetted, capering first toward Cherry and then away, teasing her but refusing to deliver, until finally he launched into a series of zany cartwheels using his enormous phallus as a pole-vaulting implement – prong, *prong*, leapfrog – with his huge hairy balls bouncing – until he receded smaller and smaller into the distance and disappeared over the horizon.

The real-life Herman kept his finger in his book and continued to observe Cherry's tossings and turnings, which had become extremely energetic. Wilder and wilder, panting and moaning, Cherry arched her blonde pubis into the air, wriggled her derriere and clenched her creamy thighs together while her fingers dived and plunged inside her honey-pot.

Suddenly the dream Herman returned, from somewhere over the horizon, looming larger and larger, running, galloping with that tremendous fire-hydrant-sized penis lurching before him, the great hairy balls jouncing up and down, the purple swollen glans caked with dirt from when he had been pronging it into the ground. Closer and closer the dream Herman loomed with his huge rod, about to plunge it up inside where Cherry wanted it.

She screamed.

"Hermannn! Herman! Now! NOW!"

She lunged, throwing herself upon him, her wet slippery fingers tracing a quick wet path across his cheek. He panicked. Flailed. His book of Edgar Guest poetry flew high into the air as he succeeded in grabbing her by her wrists and holding her off. Shaking her sternly, he yelled in her face.

"Cherry! *Cherry!* Wake up!"

She came to, moaning softly. Still under the spell of her dream, if Herman had not been holding her wrists tightly she would have reached for his penis. Herman did not let go until it was clear he was out of danger. He reached for a Kleenex and distastefully wiped his wet cheek. "You were having a *nightmare*," he told Cherry, scolding her with his tone of voice.

Perspiring heavily, Cherry fell back on her pillow with all emotion wrung out of her, though her vagina still tingled. Staring at the ceiling, she tried to gather in the threads of her receding dream. The tingles in her vagina helped. "No...Herman...I'm starting to remember. It wasn't a nightmare at all. In fact, it was very horny." And suddenly all the lucid and exciting details of her dream swept over her anew, bringing an erectness to her nipples again and a sweet pulsating current to her clitoris – making her want to tell the dream to Herman in a toned-down version so he would not call her a slut. "I dreamt you were in my arms and we were about to make love. Herman, don't get mad...we've been living together a month now and haven't consummated our relationship."

Her voice was soft and pleading, but it drove Herman into a frenzy.

"My God, Cherry! You attacked me *wantonly*. You almost *smothered* me to death!"

"But..."

"I don't understand these weird dreams of yours. It's as if you secretly *hate* me."

Her lips in a pout, Cherry's nipples went soft and her clitoris stopped throbbing and she began to feel shabby and ashamed. Tears tumbled from her eyes. Herman went on, pressing his advantage. "I've told you time and again we've got to get back to the old values. *Monogamy. Chastity.* The virtues that made America great! The America Walt Whitman *wrote* about! I don't expect too much from you at once. You need someone to give you spiritual guidance. That's why I agreed that we could live together even though we're not married. But I won't allow you to corrupt me further! Don't you see it's for your own good?"

Cherry choked back tears. Though she had a good-paying job that reflected modern attitudes brought to prominence by a hard-fought and recently won sexual revolution, and though she would certainly have been regarded as a swinger by most people, still a restrictive upbringing was not far behind her, with an unfortunate residue of old-fashioned guilt feelings that Herman was always able to use against her. The stigma of nymphomania was a thing of the past, in every place but in Cherry's mind, and she longed to establish a sexual relationship with just *one* man during off-work hours, and she wanted that man to be Herman because she loved him. He had a fine mind and a way with words, and she considered herself crude and giddy by comparison.

"Forgive me, Herman. Please...don't leave me. I got carried away. It won't happen again, I promise."

Herman snorted disdainfully, a habit of his facilitated by his perpetually swollen sinuses.

Getting out of bed, Cherry said, "I have to go. I don't want to be late."

She stood by her dressing table, brushing her hair, and shivered suddenly when a breeze from the open window caused her to feel a damp coldness between her legs, so she slipped out of her wet panties before she began to get dressed for work. Thus she did not wear any panties that morning, and it caused her to be the center of a freakish incident which I must later relate.

CHAPTER 2

Theophilus Suck loved the brand new billboard.

One hundred feet wide and seventy-five feet high, lighted at night by a combination of electronically regulated floodlights and its own luminescent paint, it stood on a high hill overlooking a main artery of the city and radiating its message daily upon the psyches of about a million commuters.

The artwork was in the form of a split screen divided diagonally by a bolt of stark yellow lightning like the lightning on Capatain Marvel's shirt, showing on the one side a voluptuous young lady with jutting breasts and dimpled buttocks being kissed a heart-rending farewell by her soldier husband or lover, his lips on hers, his fingertips touching the tips of her nipples, straining to keep touch of her till the last possible moment yet being torn from her by the speed of a fast-departing train from which he is leaning out the window like James Dean's brother Cal in the movie *East of Eden* (only Cal had to first smash his train window open with his head); while behind her back the lady of the billboard clutches in her hand her salvation and her comfort, a large flesh-colored dildo with an electric cord dangling from it; the other half of the split screen completing the tableau by showing the young lady alone later, nude in her bedroom, sitting on the edge of her bed with her legs spread, the dildo inserted where it will do the most good, a look of extreme pleasure on her face while she gazes in orgasmic rapture upon a framed photo of the recently departed soldier. The slogan of the billboard, in gigantic flaming-red letters:

YOUR FRIEND WHILE HE'S AWAY
JOYFUL NOVELTIES, INC.
MAKERS OF FINE ORGASMIC PRODUCTS
FOR THE ENTIRE FAMILY

Suck loved it because he knew it would sell. He loved it with the passion of a man who had founded his own company on the strength of a dynamic idea, and had nurtured and fed the idea until it grew into a multi-million-dollar enterprise. Joyful Novelties, Inc., was now the world's largest and best-loved supplier of erotic paraphernalia, from basic dildos to elaborately costly robot Party Dolls, largely because of the shrewdness and foresight of Theophilus Suck.

Sucretus was a Greek name, shortened at a cost of two-hundred limp worn-out dollars stained with tomato juice and the juice of other fruits and vegetables by Suck's great-grandfather, who in his immigrant's zeal to Americanize took the advice of a kindly judge who suggested that most foreigners usually shortened their names to the next nearest English word that made sense and allowed them to retain the most of the original foreign syllables. Thus, Sucretus became Suck, at a time when Suck's great-grandfather knew very little English and was inclined to lean on the advice of judges and other minor bureaucrats (with a reverential awe that did not diminish entirely even later in his career after he was paying some of them off in return for unlawful and immoral special considerations involving his operation of massage parlors, pinball emporiums and ethnic grocery stores where you could bet illegally on just about anything.)

Suck did not know his great-grandfather had come from Greece any more than he knew the shoe size of the first cave-man. He possessed a thoroughly modern lack of interest in his ancestry, his knowledge of history rooted in that collective amnesia fostered by the American school system. He could recall something about a cherry tree and for some reason he knew that George Washington had wooden teeth, but to him mostly history was a mishmash of dates except for 1492 which stood out in his brain and was irrevocably associated with Christopher Columbus and nothing else. Suck's passion to discover anything more about his origins was about as intense as the desire of a cigar-store Indian to go on a walking tour of the Soviet Union.

At age 52 Suck had a fringe of gray hair and the gray atrophied skin of one who has never taken any exercise that could be avoided. In such persons the muscles which keep their tone longest are the ones used in sitting. The eyelids sag, the paunch bloats as the abdominal muscles give way, the shoulders slump and become rounded. The mind gives its energy to schemes of commerce and acquisition, with the occasional diversion of updating a last will and testament as friends or family members fall in and out of favor.

Suck wheezed as he took in a prideful deep breath of admiration for his new billboard, while he was stuck in a massive traffic jam outside a pair of tunnels at the foot of the high hill on top of which the billboard was mounted. There were blaring horns, jammed-up cars, trucks coughing black exhaust fumes, and buses full of half-asleep people on their way to their dull jobs in the early morning.

The sun was almost done burning off the morning smog, Suck noted as he flipped on his radio and heard the following:

Good morning, this is Early Morrow, your host on DIALOGUE, sponsored by Joyful Novelties, the company that not only helps you get into your thing but helps your thing get into it. Earlier this week, the President's Commission on National Health released the startling information that we may actually be the last generation to have to die, because scientists are making remarkable strides toward understanding and defeating the aging process. In the near future, aging and dying need never take place. If so, we will be that last generation to die. We're standing by here on DIALOGUE waiting to take calls from our listeners --"

Click. Suck shut it off. It was too damned depressing. So depressing, in fact, that he did not even wait to hear the upcoming commercial for a brand-new Joyful product. He let out a sigh, and as the traffic began to crawl a little, he reached for a bottle of pills that he took daily to help him when he needed an erection.

CHAPTER 3

Meantime, about a mile back in the bumper-to-bumper fouled-up jam, Cherry Jankowski was dozing by fits and starts inside a crowded bus. Wedged in between other people, supporting herself by hanging onto a metal pole, she was trying to catch a few minutes of sound sleep while the other passengers gossiped or read newspapers or grouched and jostled at one another. She nodded, snapped awake a couple times and finally succeeded in dozing off rather soundly, and did not hear the elderly lady a few seats away from her, who was loudly disparaging a Joyful product that Cherry herself had helped test. The elderly lady was talking to another elderly lady who happened to have a brand-new dildo in a gift box sticking up out of her shopping bag. "They ought to be sued for false advertising," the complaining lady snarled. "You bought the same kind I did. Wait and see – you'll be disappointed in the orgasms."

Well, Cherry wasn't disappointed when she tested it, and if she could have heard the complaints she would have begged to differ. In other words, she would have vociferously defended the company she worked for, out of pride and loyalty.

But, as I said, Cherry was mercifully asleep. And then something disconcerting began happening. A weirdo sitting next to Cherry, with his long frazzly hair tied back in a ponytail, was being very careful not to wake Cherry up as he began pulling at the hem of her skirt, tugging at it little by little, hiking it up to reveal more and more of her creamy luscious thighs – and a lewd thrill shot through his

14

loins while his face betrayed no emotion whatsoever, when he discovered that Cherry wasn't wearing any panties.

Her absence of panties suited his intentions perfectly, as he had a small mirror taped with black electrical tape to the top of his sandal, and by positioning his foot exactly right, he maneuvered the mirror into the proper angle to enable him to see up Cherry's skirt (poor unsuspecting girl) and, sad to report, the sight of her curly blonde pubic hairs gave this ugly scoundrel a throbbing erection. A lustful gleam came to his eye and a lascivious smile to his lips as he dwelt in deep contemplation of the vagina reflected in his mirror.

(I must remark here that although this was indeed a sexually enlightened period in American history, thanks to the efforts of Theophilus Suck and other noteworthy pioneers in such matters, society still had not entirely rid itself of perverts who refused to accept the new protocols of enlightenment and decency. I am not entirely sure what this proves about the sadly persistent condition of humanity, but it surely demands further analysis and exploration.)

The bus continued onward, and the pervert glanced about stealthily and saw that no one was about to forestall his bold but sick enterprise. None of the other passengers seemed to be alarmed. And poor Cherry remained asleep. Two ladies wearing babushkas were indulging in a ribald joke-telling session with a portly well-dressed gentleman, and it is entirely possible that the crude manner of speech of these two unthinking ladies may have stimulated the freakish debauchery that I must now describe further in the interest of frank disclosure.

The weirdo with the mirror taped to his sandal slipped his hand through a premeditated hole in his trouser pocket and began to masturbate, taking just the barest pains not to betray himself, his main concern being that he wished he could shove his penis to one side so it would not rub against his cold, jaggy zipper, but he was jammed in tightly between Cherry and another passenger and could not move much without taking the mirror out of position. However, this was a minor annoyance to him, and things were going his way so well in general that he soon had the nerve to forego his masturbation for a while and to begin carefully and sneakily unfastening the buttons of Cherry's blouse. His eyes widened as he exposed her pink, delicate nipples and saw that they were in an erect state, and he deluded himself that the sleeping girl knew subconsciously that she was at the center of his erotic fantasies. But just as he began masturbating in earnest, the bus stopped with a sudden screech giving his penis a mean lurch that caused him to lose his erection.

Passengers crowded toward the exits as Cherry awakened partially numbed by sleep and pulled down her skirt and buttoned her blouse, oblivious of the fact that she had been molested. Meanwhile the pervert with the mirror on his shoe was trying desperately to keep up with her and rub his groin against her buttocks, while taking care not to have his mirror broken by someone stepping on it or stepping on it himself.

Cherry stepped down off the bus into a busy city street. Men toting briefcases ogled her, their heads dancing with visions of what they would like to do to her in bed, as the weirdo with the mirror skulked down a side street, his testicles aching with the pain of unreleased spermatic pressure.

As Cherry continued on her way, her shapely derriere undulating sweetly, naturally and inadvertently in the rhythms of sexual intercourse, she attracted the attention of a trio of hard-hatted construction workers carrying metal lunch buckets, and they whistled at her and yelled suggestive obscenities. Cherry did her best to ignore them, but turned crimson from embarrassment.

It happened that an old man wearing a long black coat was rummaging in a garbage can, hoping to find something to eat so he could save his last fifty cents for a small glass of cheap wine. He fished and fished and came up with a lovely morsel – almost half a fish sandwich with ketchup. But on spying Cherry his fingers separated involuntarily and his meal dropped back into the can, one half of the bun coming loose and falling amongst the rotted garbage while the other half remained stuck to the fish.

But no matter. The old duffer had other fish to fry.

With his red eyes glued on Cherry's pouting lips, his grizzled Adam's apple bobbing every time he swallowed, he waited till the sweet girl got within six feet of him, then opened the flaps of his coat, exposing himself. He exhibited his flaccid penis and sagging scrotum, sagging the way they tend to sag when men get old, as also the cartilage in their ears tends to relax, making their ears larger. Cherry took note of the old duffer's cleverness, though: he had snipped away the lower part of his dirty shirt and tie so that they stopped halfway down his chest, and his "trousers" were merely the legs of trousers fastened with elastic around his upper thighs, all to facilitate the exhibiting of his privates at a moment's notice, after which he could take to his heels and lose himself in a crowd if the occasion demanded it.

Although his getup was interesting and innovative, Cherry kept a straight face, tilting her nose in the air and passing him by without giving undue encouragement to his bad habit.

"Don't worry, sister!" he yelled after her. "You ain't gettin' *this* big tool! Eat your *heart* out!" And he closed the flaps of his coat solemnly and protectively around his penis as if he were saving it for a special event. Cherry was not naive in such matters, and she figured that he was probably saving it for masturbation.

She walked about three more blocks and entered a modern brick and glass building bearing the neon sign and logo of Joyful Novelties, Inc. A young female receptionist gave a casual nod from behind her desk as Cherry smiled cheerfully and said good morning.

At the far end of a corridor, Theophilus Suck, fully clothed, was engaged in a very serious conversation with a naked young man named Marcello Fettucini. Marcello was quite handsome, and had been told often of his resemblance to an Italian movie star whose first name was also Marcello. He sported a thick black mustache and a good-sized penis, 7.73 inches long and 1.65 inches in diameter when erect, according to his Joyful Product Tester Personnel Profile. But he seemed at the moment to be demoralized about something. He kept nervously shifting his weight from one foot to the other and glancing down at his inert penis. Suck was staring at Marcello with his hands on his hips, as if words had just been spoken in anger and more were to follow.

Entering the corridor, Cherry heard Suck's whiny sing-song voice and it startled her. She stopped in her tracks and listened, refraining from poking her head around the corner.

"Marcello, you're a sad case, my boy! I don't know what I'm going to do with you. I hate to fire you, but your performance of late is pathetic. Ten erection failures in one month! You used to be one of our very best product testers, but now all you've got is a limp noodle!"

Marcello gulped, and Suck went on. "Your failures have become locker-room gossip. You're costing this company money. And all our employees take a hit because of our profit-sharing incentive. I can't keep you on here if you won't perform. I'm trying to be fair but..."

Marcello stammered, "I - I - I donna know what's-a wrong. Maybe I'm inna a - a *slump*. Maybe I'm not-a eating right!"

(Marcello had an Italian accent, and spoke in broken English – a chore for me to duplicate in print. But I will do my best, dear reader.)

"Please, I will-a try harder," Marcello said.

"I want you to *get* harder, not just try harder," Suck said. He shook his head exasperatingly and went into his office and slammed the door. Marcello stared at the slammed door, then shrugged his shoulders and scratched his head and looked despairingly at his limp penis as he moped down the long hallway that led to the locker room and the main testing laboratory.

Cherry stared pityingly after him. Like all the product testers at Joyful, she had heard about his problem. He could not get it up anymore. A tragic fate for any young man, but especially for one whose bread and butter is dependent upon his ability to perform daily and hourly. Marcello seemed to be washed up. Cherry had heard the other product testers heckling him in the lunch room and shower room; many of them had no respect for one who had fallen, and Suck encouraged this attitude because he believed, perhaps erroneously, that most people put out hardest when under pressure. His product testers were expected to deliver orgasm after orgasm in the relentless testing and perfecting of Joyful products.

Cherry stepped out of the corridor into a locker room where there were several young ladies in various stages of undress. A woman named Betty, nude except for a bra with smiling yellow faces on it, tried to smile at Cherry but failed because of her hangover. Her lips were so dry, cracked and dehydrated that she managed only a sort of croak when she said, "Cherry, please, can I have some of your aspirins?"

Another woman, who had removed all her clothing and was stepping into a pair of red high-heeled shoes, turned to Cherry and said, "How was your weekend?"

"Fine," Cherry replied somewhat disingenuously.

"Get laid?" the woman said with a snicker.

And a third woman, applying petroleum jelly to her labia while the cigarette clenched between her lips higher up dropped ashes on her breasts, gestured at the one with the hangover and said, "Poor Betty, she had another bad weekend." But there was no trace of sympathy in her voice, just a cold, biting statement of pure fact. She wiped her fingers with a tissue and threw it in the wastebasket.

A fourth woman, sitting on the toilet douching, looked up at everybody and laughed for no apparent reason.

Cherry got her locker open and began to dig for the aspirins while hung-over Betty took off her smiling bra and sat on a bench, moaning and holding her head. She said, "I have to be drunk before I can ball my old man – or *anybody* for that matter. I'm losing my mind. What's *wrong* with me?"

"No more aspirins," Cherry announced, holding up the empty bottle.

"Oh shit, how'm I gonna *work*?" Betty lamented, puckering her face up as though she might cry or vomit.

But the lady with ashes on her tits merely laughed in a coarse manner and uttered a trite sarcasm thatr a more charitable person would have left unsaid: "My heart is *bleeding* for you."

The woman who was douching laughed. And the lady in the red shoes, who was now standing by the sink and looking in the mirror as she lathered her public hair and began to shave, turned to Cherry and asked, "What're you testing today?"

"I don't know," Cherry replied. "I didn't read the schedule."

The woman with ashes on her tits said angrily, "I'm testing another goddamn *dildo*!" And she took another tissue and wiped excess petroleum jelly from her labia.

"Oh my god!" hung-over Betty griped. "Don't any of us ever get a real *prick* around here?"

"A real prick? What's that?" ashes on her tits said.

"Something my mother told me about," said the one shaving her public area, as she rinsed her razor under the tap.

"You shoulda seen the contraption I tested last Thursday," Hung-over Betty said. "A spittin' image of a Colt .45 with the barrel in the shape of a penis – for douching. It's called The Peacemaker. You pull the trigger and it squirts lemon juice."

"I nicked myself! Ouch!" said the lady who had been shaving, and she ripped off a piece of toilet paper and tried to use it to stanch the flow of blood.

"You should thank your lucky stars," the lady with ashes on her tits said to Hung-over Betty. "Last Friday I was scheduled for a test with Marcello Fettucini, the Great Italian Lover! What an exercise in futility!"

"He used to be so hot-blooded," the lady who had been shaving said as she dabbed at the razor nick on her labia.

"Forget it, he's washed up," the lady with ashes on her tits said. "I wouldn't be surprised to see him playing bocce with the old men at the Sons of Italy."

"He's a worn-out stud," Hung-over Betty scoffed. "I've seen plenty of 'em come and go around here. No skin off *my* ass!"

Cherry had a pensive look on her face as she donned a white lab coat over her lithe, naked body. She couldn't help wondering: If she continued to work at Joyful, would she turn out as jaded and callous as the other ladies? She certainly hoped not. She was only going to work there long enough to put Herman through college. And he would get his poems published. And he would marry her. And they would live happily together, with the past behind them. All of her hopes and dreams were focused on Herman, and she was willing to work hard to be his helpmate and to help him succeed. Deep inside she was the kind of girl any man would cherish.

CHAPTER 4

Inside a plush conference room, Theophilus Suck sipped orange juice and admired the display racks and showcases designed to show off the entire line of Joyful products in an appealing, eye-catching fashion. Assorted whips, chains, dildos, vibrators, simulated vaginas, and so forth, were exhibited as attractively as possible in a panorama executed by a top-flight industrial display house, and each item was accompanied by an ad-agency blurb describing its application and benefits. It might be well to list some of these products, for the enlightenment of those few readers who may be unfamiliar with the Joyful line. The following items, excerpted at random, may also be found in the Joyful Novelties catalogue:

The Whing-Dinger. Joyful's deluxe nine-inch penis reproduction with a built-in vibrator which creates an out-of-this world sensation on both penis and vagina during sexual intercourse. Priced at an economical $29.95 it is easily within reach of the most modest budget.

The Delay-Lay. A sheath of soft latex rubber with a firm rubber tip that fits over the penis, extending its length by two inches and allowing the male to delay his climax by slightly dulling the sensations in the glans. $20 apiece, two for $30.

Crown Royale. A rubber device to extend the "crown" of the penis, it fits on the organ directly behind the corona (the rounded ridge behind the head). The two tiny bulbs are filled with air and simulate the firmness of the erect organ, thus treating any woman to the massive penetration she craves. The kit contains one large-bulbed extension, one medium, at an easy-to-afford $23.95.

The Speed King. A penis extender with built-in ticklers in the form of dozens of tiny little latex fingers to comb and curry the inside of her vagina, guaranteed to trigger off those legendary multiple orgasms. Really worth it at $27.95. Smaller sizes are priced slightly lower.

The Helping Hand. Designed to reproduce the sensations normally provided to the male organ inside the vagina. This is the one artificial vagina that can pass the blindfold test. The muscle surrounding the entrance to the vagina is simulated by the rubber bulb, which may be rhythmically contracted during use. Can be inflated with either air or warm water. A bargain at $35.

Big John. You'll swear it's real when you're using it, but oh boy what a whang! Nineteen inches long and a full three inches in diameter, this simulated penis is made of soft rubber, very lifelike, with two heavy hanging balls which may be filled with warm water or milk and squeezed to simulate ejaculation at the desired moment. The best money can buy, at $37.95.

The Slave Queen. Make her your slave! This item comes in three sections: an iron collar with lock and key and two breast chains which may be attached to the collar. The breast chains may then be tightened and locked to compress the breasts at their base, making them seem larger and subjecting her to your total domination. With two horse whips thrown in, it can be yours for only $50.

Party Doll. For those who need something more stimulating than a teddy bear! Made of soft inflatable vinyl, she feels like actual live flesh. Life-sized, blonde, and really stacked: 38-24-36. (See color photo above.) You can pack her up and take her anywhere. She never says no.

Great for gags or just plain good company. She can be yours for just $49.95, direct from the Joyful warehouse.

This is just a sampling of many terrific items that formed the backbone of Theophilus Suck's Joyful Novelty company. They were all of good, sturdy, functional construction, backed up by years of research and development. Into each product was built a certain degree of planned obsolescence, but for the ones listed above there was a good steady demand that helped the Company achieve a stable level of guaranteed monthly sales, even while more exotic innovations were being tested and marketed.

The testing of new product – the sort of work performed daily by product testers like Cherry Jankowski and Marcello Fettucini (when he was capable) – was an integral and highly important component of the Joyful Novelties structure. And Theophilus Suck, as he sipped his orange juice, shook his head over how proud he was of his product testers when they performed well, and how much he shared their misery when they suffered malfunctions of the body and spirit. He felt that he was not a coldhearted taskmaster, but a kind and benevolent father figure whose pioneering efforts had given them rewarding careers and gainful employment.

CHAPTER 5

The Chief Engineer of Test Lab #5 held an unrolled green condom gingerly between the thumb and forefinger of his left hand. The Male Tester and Female Tester stood totally nude before him awaiting their instructions, as Joyful engineers and aides scurried about, trying to act busy even if they were not, and performing last-minute checks on various pieces of test equipment.

"As you can see," the Chief Engineer said, "this brand-new Joyful prophylactic combines both visual and tactile appeal for the discerning consumer. We plan to market an entire line of condoms in assorted colors, called Joyful Rainbow Rubbers, combining eye-appeal and unusual strength and thinness in a design that is aimed at the desire for novelty that is characteristic of older marriages."

The Female Tester was trying to pay attention, but her clitoris was already moist and tingling because the Male Tester happened to be one that she fancied. She smiled at him, rubbed against him, and gave a gentle tug on his penis, which began to stiffen.

"Of course," the Chief Engineer added, "we feel that the option for many and varied colors in a condom should also excite the flamboyant impetuosity of younger people."

The Female Tester was now kissing the Male Tester playfully on the ear, while he had begun to massage her breasts, skilfully pinching the nipples now and again or brushing them lightly, subtly, with the hairs on the back of his hand. The Male Tester's penis had risen to almost a full erection. Of course it would have been totally erect, throbbing and ready to ejaculate, had he been a mere callow youth and inexperienced.

A Joyful engineer, thumbing through a sheaf of papers on a clipboard, came over and said, "We are interested in how this condom feels and how it performs; in other words slippage and breakage. So far it has performed satisfactorily in its machine tests; now it must be subjected to the human factor."

The Female Tester had gotten to her knees and was licking the Male Tester's testicles. She sucked on each testicle in its turn, then traced a path with her tongue along the ridge of the penis to the glans, which she continued to lick with the tip of her tongue, while she gripped the sturdy shaft in one hand and squeezed the testicles with her other hand. And the male tester, doing his part conscientiously, kept both his hands busy massaging the Female Tester's breasts, while she slipped her fingers inside her warm, wet vagina and rubbed her clitoris.

"Hold it! Hold it right there!" the Company Photographer exclaimed as he stepped up and began snapping pictures, his flash strobing and flashing. "Lick the tip of his cock again," he said. "Let me get a few glamour shots for the Annual Report."

The Chief Engineer picked up a box of Joyful Rainbow Rubbers and handed it to the Male Tester. Then he stopped in his tracks, grinned modestly, and inquired of the Photographer, "Want me to clear your shot, Sam?"

"No, no, not at all. You're fine. I've got everything I need. I'll get some more shots when you start the actual testing."

"We need good coverage on this," the Marketing Director said.

"We're almost ready to begin," said the Chief Engineer. He turned to the Male Tester, who was now having his penis sucked in earnest and was now approaching the point where heeding directions would be difficult, even though all product testers had been chosen for their ability to do what they were told even under extreme passion, and to maintain erections and erotic enthusiasm even while listening to technical instructions. "Put this on as you would any other condom," the Chief Engineer explained. "It's a fresh one, right off the assembly line. Do not attempt to restrict movement during intercourse. We'll be checking, testing, measuring its performance under stress. Afterward, we will want both of you present at the scheduled critique session."

The Female Tester now had a firm grip on the Male Tester's buttocks and was working his penis in and out of her mouth from the tip to the base, plunging it as deep as it would go, withdrawing it to barely retain contact with her extended tongue, simulating the plunges and thrusts of a penis inside a vagina, her lips employing a sucking, tugging action that left the shaft coated with saliva.

The Male Tester withdrew his rock-hard penis from the Female Tester's mouth, and an alert aide rushed over with a towel to wipe it dry as the Male Tester opened the package he had been handed and took out a rolled-up condom. It happened to be a lime-colored one, lubricated, with a nipple reservoir. As usual, the Male Tester had to force it over the swollen glans of his penis, but after the initial difficulty it went on easily enough and resulted in a snug, comfortable fit.

The Female Tester looked up with a glassy-eyed smile and cupped the Male Tester's scrotum in the palm of her hand. The two embraced and tumbled onto the bed, and one of the assistant engineers pressed a button, causing the bed to rise pneumatically, with a buzzing electrical sound, to the proper height for scientific observation.

The Chief Engineer double-checked the oscilloscope screen and the various gauges and dials, as electrodes were connected to the proper places on the bodies of the Male Tester and the Female Tester. A team of engineers gathered around the elevated bed and leaned in to observe and take notes, armed with clipboards, stethoscopes, thermometers and other testing and measuring equipment unfamiliar to the layman but impressive in its array of wires, tubes and gadgetry.

The Company Photographer began snapping pictures once again. And the Video Crew went into action, getting good dramatic close-ups of the fornication, which would be later scored with light music and made into cassettes to be marketed under the brand name of Joyful Pornographic Pleasures, sold in department stores throughout America, for home enjoyment.

The Chief Engineer observed closely as the Male Tester inserted his penis in the Female Tester's vagina and an Aide took hold of the shaft of the penis at its base to ascertain whether or not the Joyful Rainbow Rubber had slipped any during these initial moments. Upon insertion, another Aide pushed a button on his stopwatch and the seconds began to tick away.

"We're going to take readings on the amount of time to climax for each of you," the Chief Engineer explained, "to be compared to your average time while using a regular condom. This particular model, in addition to the innovation of the color scheme, has been packaged in a light lubricating oil that should delay climax. Let us know when you reach orgasm."

"Enjoy yourselves as usual, an Assistant Engineer admonished. "But keep in mind the purpose of these tests. Try to strain the condom to its breaking point. If it refuses to rupture despite the most grueling treatment you can give it, we'll know that the tensile strength is superb."

"It's still very secure," an Aide announced as he once again seized the shaft of the Male Tester's penis and checked for slippage. An assistant listened with his stethoscope to the heartbeats of the Male Tester and the Female Tester and made notes on one of his charts.

The Audio Engineer tuned the volume of his headset as he listened to the slipping and sliding noises of the penis inside the vagina while, oblivious to it all, the Male Tester and the Female Tester continued fornicating for all they were worth, concentrating on giving the company a good return for their day's wages, and proceeding rapidly toward the point of orgasm.

CHAPTER 6

Cherry Jankowski and Theophilus Suck were talking in hushed tones just outside a closed door at the end of a brightly illuminated hallway. The hallway was lined with portraits of notable Joyful product testers, male and female, who in past years had earned praise and recognition for their remarkable endurance, or their spirit of self-sacrifice, or their pioneering efforts in being the first to test new and wonderful Joyful products. Suck had chosen this site to talk with Cherry because he wanted something from her and he needed to fire up her sense of pride and company loyalty.

After he confided in her, she stammered, "But what am I supposed to do about it - I - I—"

"Shhh!" Suck said, touching his fingers to his lips. "Marcello will hear you. He's right inside the room."

"I'm sorry," Cherry whispered, her face reddening.

"Once upon a time," Suck said, "Marcello was one of the best product testers Joyful ever had. A typical hot-blooded dago. I was sure that when he retired, one of these days, his portrait would take its place alongside all of these others!"

"I don't know if I can help him," Cherry said. "I'd like to, but..."

Suck looked her in the eyes. *"Your* portrait can be up here someday, Cherry. You have what it takes, and you're coming along very well. Don't think I haven't noticed. I'm very *proud* of you! I'll have to fire Marcello if someone can't turn him on – or at least cause him to show some improvement."

31

"No, don't fire him," Cherry said. "That would be awful!"

"Then it's up to you. The responsibility is on your shoulders. Will you give it the old college try?"

"Well...yes," said Cherry. "Yes...I suppose so..." Caught in a moral dilemma which was too complex for her, she worried about whether or not she would be doing the right thing. She usually could not figure such things out on her own, and needed Herman to advise her. Poor girl. Although she was decent enough, she was a product of a society with no absolute moral values, and as a result she was always just a little confused.

"You'll come through with flying colors," Suck said. "If anyone can turn him on, you must be the one. That body of yours could give an erection to an Egyptian mummy."

Cherry turned absolutely crimson. The compliment from her boss pleased her, but it also disturbed her because it was one more instance of someone liking her physically rather than intellectually, and Herman had told her that true love and admiration were products of the intellect rather than the base emotions. Nevertheless, she put her hand on the door knob and steeled herself to do battle with Marcello's terrible affliction. Suck winked at her and said, "Just think! You won't have to test a thing! This one is *on the company*!"

Now that she thought of it *that* way, her spirits picked up. She was going to be allowed to fornicate on company time, maybe, if Marcello didn't punk out on her, and she would not have to worry about what the Joyful engineers wanted her to do and how they wanted her to do it, and she would not be tangled up in wires and electrodes. She could even pretend she was having sex with Herman. Lost in these delightful anticipations, she entered the room rather briskly and closed the door, inadvertently slamming it too hard and startling Marcello, whose numbed brain had been occupied in the unhappy task of trying to think of a way to commit suicide by a painless yet dignified method. He looked up at Cherry with a forlorn expression that immediately won her sympathy. He was sitting on the edge of a bunk bed in a soft glow of light from a lamp on an end table which also supported a bottle of bourbon, an ice bucket and two glasses. These accouterments were the most romantic that Suck had been able to devise on the spur of the moment.

Cherry came over to the bed and poured a shot of bourbon for Marcello, who did not dare look up as she wiggled out of her white lab coat and allowed it to drop at her feet. Insecurity in the presence of a beautiful woman was a feeling which was brand new to him. He raised his eyes slowly, taking in the voluptuousness of her and trembling slightly. She sat next to him, brushing against him, as he gulped down his bourbon, making his eyes smart, and wiped his lips with the back of his hand as she wet her lips with the tip of her tongue and leaned toward him. She tugged at the hair on his chest, then kissed each of his nipples, running her tongue lightly over them while she took his penis in her hand, fondling it, noting the size of it soft and thinking what a tremendous whang it must be, if she could only get it up for him.

She commenced blowing in his ear, then giving him light kisses on his shoulders, his neck, his back, the base of his spine and his buttocks. "What-a are you doing?" he asked nervously, and realized how stupid the question was, as Cherry began running the tip of her tongue from his navel to his groin area. "Relax, Marcello...just relax," she said in a whisper of soft, sensuous encouragement.

"You are-a wasting your time," he said, his voice tight with anguish,

A thrill shot through her because of his Italian accent, as she took his penis in her mouth. He grimaced, showing his bad teeth, but Cherry did not see them because she was otherwise employed.

"Mama mia," he said, his voice laden with despair, as Cherry sucked at the head of his penis, running her tongue around it coaxingly and drawing on it with excited little licks and nibbles. "I give-a the best-a years of my life to this-a company," he said embarrassedly, "and all I have-a to show for it is a limp-a pecker."

His rubbery soft penis flopped out of her mouth when she drew back to examine the results of her efforts, noting that if it had gotten any larger, she was unable to detect it with her naked eye. Because the situation was so frustrating, she was having difficulty staying interested. "Relax," she said. "You're just uptight." And she slipped her warm, wet tongue inside Marcello's navel as she moved her hands to the erogenous zone just behind his testicles and kneaded the large muscle there.

"Once I was-a the biggest stud in-a town," Marcello blurted defensively.

Cherry lay her cheek against his navel, ready to listen if he wanted to talk about his problem.

"The others say I am-a washed up. They rejoice in-a my misfortune. They gloat and tell-a me to my face that I am ready for the, how you say...glue factory."

Cherry lay still, her face pressed against his flat, muscular, hairy Italian belly. "I don't believe what they say," she stated earnestly. "I think you've got a lot of spunk in you."

"Mama mia!" Marcello said with a long, agonizing sigh, and as Cherry felt his strong chest heaving, it was inconceivable to her that such a fine body was incapable of producing an erection. Involuntarily, her tongue flicked out and make contact with the head of his penis and once more her mouth closed around it. She began pulling at it with her lips, the way a bird tugs a worm out of the ground, and she found herself enjoying the elastic give and pull of it – which she hoped was not going to last very long, however, because her clitoris was throbbing and she was getting intensely excited. She was thinking how good Marcello's 7.73 inch penis was going to feel inside her, ramming and prodding, with no Joyful engineers telling them how to go about it.

But it was not to be.

Marcello brought things to a rude halt by grabbing her by her wrists and pulling her up so he could look her right in her eyes. "Who put-a you uppa to this?" he demanded. And she noted that his accent got worse when he was angry.

"No one," she lied.

"Someone putta you up to this," Marcello insisted. "Suck – was it Suck? Bafongool!" And he smacked his right bicep with his left hand.

Cherry lunged at him and tried to kiss him but he pushed her away. "I know Suck putta you uppa to this," he said. "He don't-a like to lose money. I once worked three days overtime for-a him without falling down onna the job."

Remembering his past glory, he let go of Cherry and stared up at the ceiling, letting out a long, anguished sigh. "I try everything to help-a my myself," he murmured. "I try health foods, how you say...aphrodisiacs...I even try eating bulls' balls from-a Mexico. I try Spanish fly. Nothing does-a no good!"

Suddenly he jumped and grabbed Cherry by her shoulders and stared at her with a wild, desperate look in his eyes. "If you really want-a to help-a me," he pleaded passionately, "you must-a tell Suck a lie. Tell-a him we made love. Tell-a him I'm all right, so I won't have-a to lose my job."

She nodded her head weakly. She found herself gazing into his eyes, her own eyes moist with empathy and good intentions. "I'd *like* to help you," she said meekly.

"Then do as-a I say," he told her. "It is-a the only way. If I canna getta my head together, I save-a some lira...I mean, dollars...I go back-a to Roma. I die inna the land of my birth."

He could not help trying to make her pity him, a tactic he had used to charm so many women in the past. Even though his penis was useless, his mouth kept pouring out the right words to make a woman fall in love. It was a habit and a talent that had proved very useful, once upon a time. He let out another of his long sighs. And despite his awful plight, his eyes stayed on Cherry's lovely body as she put her lab coat back on and left the room. When the door closed, his mind dwelt on memories of her dimpled buttocks and long, shapely thighs and calves. Her breasts also were more than satisfactory, but he had always been what in popular jargon is termed "a leg and ass man." Perhaps, he thought, there could be a tidbit of hope in the fact that he had not yet totally lost his aesthetic appreciation for items of feminine beauty. Maybe he might yet find his way out of the morass of his predicament.

If not, he might truly take the easy way out.

CHAPTER 7

Cherry told Theophilus Suck the lie she had promised to Marcello. She felt guilty about lying, and Suck of course did not believe her, but he said nothing to indicate this as she backed out of his office awkwardly, nervously, and closed the door.

Suck was amused by the power he had over her. He let out a sigh for his lost youth, which he had spent reading the *Wall Street Journal* and opening chains of pornographic movie houses, instead of pursuing delectable young things like Cherry Jankowski, and now that he had the power to have any girl he wanted, he no longer had the will or the energy. The memory of sexual electricity coursing through his veins and nerve endings was a phenomenon he could intellectualize but not *feel* any longer, as a man can look at a photo of himself as a baby and realize that he definitely *was* a baby at one time, yet he has no idea of what being a baby *feels* like. At age 52, Theophilus Suck was for all practical purposes totally impotent; that is, he had an occasional erection but not when he willed himself to have one and not with enough consistency and dependability to make plans. This was not the most gratifying condition for a man who bossed a company that surrounded him hour upon hour with every type of fornication imaginable. He hoped that his secret failing was not known by anyone except himself and his wife, who of course could not be kept from knowing and eventually had to be told in no uncertain terms, so she would at least know to leave him alone.

37

A part of Suck hoped that Marcello did not recover, even though Marcello's powers at their peak had been good for business. It made Suck's heart glad in some mysterious way to watch the sexual downfall of a much younger man who had every reason to be stock full of vim and vigor. A gloating smile came to Suck's thin lips when he thought of how he had lambasted Marcello verbally in the hallway at the beginning of the work day, intentionally knocking the pins out from under him before he could even get started. The mental pressures Marcello was under had been of sufficient weight to prevent him from responding to a sexpot like Cherry Jankowski, even under good romantic conditions. Suck knew exactly what had gone on between Cherry and Marcello when they were alone in that room, because it was rigged for electronic surveillance, set up that way by a private eye who had once escaped serving time for his part in the famous Watergate scandal of the 1970s. The room had several hidden microphones and two concealed video cameras.

Suck chuckled out loud as he reached absently for a vibrator of a new and radical design which was lying in his file tray. He clicked it on and listened to the hum of its tiny motor. He especially liked to tinker with the new products. He had no doubt that he would fire Marcello when it pleased him to do so. But for the time being he was enjoying toying with his former top product tester. Pleased with himself, he lowered his hand under his desk and touched the whirring vibrator to his groin area, rubbing and pressing it against his trousers. No stirrings down there, as expected. Damn it. He clicked the vibrator off to avoid running down the battery. The batteries weren't long-lasting, on purpose. Suck wanted folks to have to replace them frequently so he'd have a chance of selling more of them in his stores.

CHAPTER 8

Driving home from work in her Volkswagen Beetle, Cherry Jankowski was filled with pride when the Top Forty station on her car radio ran a commercial for the Joyful Novelties Whing-Dinger, a product she had tested! She could recall the joy it had given her in the laboratory and the glowing report she had given to the Joyful engineers. Even now, thinking about it made her tingle.

She got out of the Beetle, loaded herself down with bags of groceries, and entered the foyer of her apartment building, where Mr. Stag the janitor was busy sweeping. The floor was always pretty clean, but somehow he always needed to sweep a lot around Cherry's apartment. She appreciated it. She assumed he did the same for all the other tenants and so she considered him a very conscientious janitor, which was not the case.

He looked up, and stuttered, "H-h-hey, Ch-Ch-Cherry b-baby, When y-you g-g-gonna g-gimme a l-little t-t-t-twat?"

"Mr. Stag! You should be ashamed of yourself!"

He stood looking after Cherry with his broom and dustpan as she scampered up the stairs. He would have bent over and tried to peek up her skirt, but the banister and railing blocked his view.

Stag was not physically attractive, but that did not curb his desire to jab his penis into a pretty girl, any more than poverty stops a poor man from desiring a Rolls Royce. He had warts all over his face, caused by a Vitamin A deficiency which stood no chance of being ameliorated because he called anyone who took vitamins a health nut. And he also had a red bulbous nose with all the capillaries burst in it, caused by drinking too much because of the warts, and he resented the fact that these unfortunate blemishes would probably keep him from ever having sex with a girl as pretty as Cherry. She was the prettiest girl he had ever seen, and he shouted at her as she stood on the landing, "H-h-hey, Ch-Cherry, m-m-maybe I d-d-don't t-turn you on b-but I'll t-tell your one thing, I b-b-bet I g-got a b-b-bigger whang than a l-lot of these s-s-s-sissified d-dudes with their f-faggoty l-long hair and b-b-beads and earrings. You'd b-b-b-be d-doin' yourself a f-favor if you'd t-take a t-t-tumble in the s-sack with m-m-me."

By the time he got it all out, Cherry's attention had wandered and she missed the point of what he was saying, so she merely replied absently, "We'll see, Mr. Stag." Which caused his heart to leap with a tinge of hope as she shifted her bags of groceries and fumbled through her purse for her keys.

After gazing up at her for a long while, Stag stepped under the stairwell, out of sight of anyone who might enter the building all of a sudden, and took out his penis and played with it till he had a throbbingly huge erection. He kept playing with it, bringing himself to the threshold of ejaculation quite a few times, so as to prolong the pleasure and to make his penis get as large as possible. Then he reached into his bib pocket for a carpenter's rule which he always carried with him, and unfolded it and measured his penis from base to tip. Nine inches on the nose.

It was Stag's pride and torment that he had a penis probably bigger than any other in the apartment complex, yet he was always being turned down by Cherry and all the other luscious teeny-boppers and housewives. Because of his warts and bulbous red nose and the self-consciousness they fostered which in turn caused him to stutter, the sexual revolution had not lavished any benefits in his direction. But he remained convinced that if he could ever get Cherry or any of the others to go to bed with him, his tremendous implement would do such a startlingly fine job that his reputation would be made and he would be in like Flynn from then on.

Meanwhile Cherry had found her keys and was trying one of them in the lock when suddenly the door to the next-door apartment flew open and Mr. Biggs poked his head out and unzipped his fly and waved his erect penis at her. Then he stepped back inside like a bird popping in and out of a cuckoo clock, and in his own privacy, his lusts all fired up with thoughts of diddling Cherry, he seized an empty orange juice bottle from under the sink and inserted his penis into it and pumped and pumped, grunting and sighing, until he ejaculated. He even reached back and slapped himself smartly on the buttocks at the moment of climax. Then he waited for his erection to diminish, but the blood vessels were unfortunately constricted by the neck of the bottle, keeping the organ so engorged that it would not go down.

Biggs had not encountered this particular problem before, and it had him perplexed and mortified. He began peeling off the label of the bottle, scraping at it with his fingernails, in an effort to obtain an unobstructed view of his organ so he could determine just what was the matter. The fact that he was able to react so calmly and intelligently shows his ability to keep his wits about him in a situation that might have caused others to panic.

Unaware of all this drama, Cherry sighed and let herself into her apartment.

CHAPTER 9

Now I fear that I must digress, much as I hate to disturb the flow of this story and your deep involvement with its characters. This digression is for the benefit of those slow-witted readers who need guideposts before they can understand a thing properly. In other words, they need someone else to do their thinking for them.

I therefore wish to point out in no uncertain terms that this is not a pornographic novel. If it were, the people in it would have no problems except superficial ones, and they would cheerfully wend their way from one carnal episode into another. The reader could justly expect to receive a substantial measure of erotic titillation on just about every page. But instead, the characters in this book are, almost without exception, laboring under difficulties of such extreme mental and physical duress that it would be a callous reader indeed who could overcome his feelings of empathy and pathos sufficiently to become titillated by anything on these humble pages. No, it ought to be clear that this is a novel that deals with the serious, weighty themes which have absorbed philosophers and playwrights throughout the centuries, from Euripides to Mamet. It asks deep questions such as:

Where are we going? What are we headed for? Is all not quite right with our newfound sexual freedom?

In order to deal with these weighty matters, I have had to be explicit and honest. I have not shrunk from describing acts of others which are unsavory, lewd and sometimes actually reprehensible, where such things had to be described in order to carry out the plot and theme of this ambitious work. There are doubtless some few readers base enough to derive erotic stimulation from such passages.

This grieves me as much as it grieves anyone, yet such aggravations are the lot of the honest writer who seeks to portray things as they are, not as they should be, thereby pointing the way toward what we may become. I firmly believe that to shrink from revealing the whole truth and nothing but the truth would be an awful distortion and would cheat you of the knowledge you need in order to make proper evaluation of the people and events I have chosen to boldly portray. That's exactly why I have taken a forthright, open stance in presenting the substance of this book. I am prepared to be criticized, even vilified, in some circles, knowing full well that such is often the reward of those who shun hypocrisy. But I go to bed each night with a clean literary conscience. And if I keep my dignity, even if I lose all else, I shall count myself a lucky man.

CHAPTER 10

Herman Longfellow looked up from his typewriter as Cherry walked across the living room with her bags of groceries. It was apparent to her that he had been hard at work all day, typing his fingers to the bone, trying to complete his collection of poetry which they were both hoping to see published.

But, as is often the case in this life, what was apparent was not true; for example, although it is "apparent" that the world is flat, this has been found out not to be so. Thus, Herman had not been typing all afternoon, though he very much wanted Cherry to think that. You will recall that earlier, without making a big deal out of it, I made mention of the fact that Herman was a transvestite. I have no problem with it, of course; it is largely his own business. But I do think that it truly *is* a factor that Cherry ought to have been told, because it would have helped her more accurately assess their relationship. Herman should have been more honest. He should have given Cherry a fair chance to accept or reject a platonic relationship if he felt it was the best he could offer.

In any case, he had spent most of the afternoon dressing up and admiring himself, primping and promenading in black bra and frilly panties and open-toed high-heeled shoes in front of a full-length mirror in Cherry's bedroom. Then he had masturbated while watching *Hollywood Squares* and *The Dating Game*. By the time he heard Cherry outside trying her key in the lock, he had all the female clothes put away, inside his typewriter case, and was posed innocently in front of the typewriter.

"My new poem is coming along very nicely," he announced, in order to heighten the illusion that he had been working.

"Oh, Herman, I'm so glad to hear it!" Cherry exclaimed. She set her bags of groceries on the dining-room table and began taking things out and putting them away.

"It was an inspiration," Herman added. "It practically wrote itself."

"I'm so dumb compared to you," Cherry said. "I don't know why you love me." She cast her eyes downward, cowed by the tremendous weight of her own ignorance, and Herman did not say anything to dissuade her feelings of inferiority because they helped keep her meek and under his control.

"Herman?"

"Yes, dear?"

"I love you, honey. And I'm sorry about this morning. My erotic dream and all. It was a disgusting thing for me to do. I mean, you're the only one who isn't always trying to get in my pants, and I ought to appreciate it more. It's my fault for letting my lusts get the better of me. You're right. You're right about everything."

It was the most she had ever said to Herman in one burst, and it drained her. She felt emotionally pooped but tremendously unburdened as she turned away from Herman with a lump in her throat and reached for a jar of Heinz pickles and tried to find room for them in the refrigerator. The fridge was too small, but it came with the apartment.

"We've lost the simplicity and repose of life," Herman said. This was a direct quote from Samuel Clemens, but Herman always allowed Cherry to think that everything he said was original; therefore he did not attribute the quote. And Cherry was so impressed with it that she paused in mid-air with a can of Hershey's chocolate that she had been about to move to make room for the Heinz pickles, and when she tried to put the can of chocolate down, it stuck to her hand.

"I have to work overtime tonight," she said. "Mr. Suck asked me and I accepted. We need the extra money."

She peeled her hand from the sticky can and went to the sink to wipe both hand and can with a wet dishcloth. Herman was always so sloppy with ketchup and syrup and anything that came in a bottle. She looked at him out of the corner of her eye, but didn't want to say anything to upset him because she didn't want him to complain about her having to work overtime. But she needn't have worried. The money Cherry earned at Joyful was exceedingly important to Herman. Money was a thing his artistic temperament did not cause him to eschew. He felt it was Cherry's duty to provide him with physical sustenance and material comforts, thereby freeing his mind for fugues and rhapsodies of poetic beauty. He had a goal and a purpose, in his life and in his art. He tranquilly accepted everything about himself, including his transvestism, which he thought of as a delightful eccentricity, akin to Shelley's occasional quirky habit of coming totally nude into a drawing room full of Victorian socialites. Herman sometimes thought of himself as a sort of neo-Emily Dickinson, in that through metaphorical exploration of microcosms, his poetry, like hers, was destined to reveal something large about the workings of the universe.

Both Herman and Cherry were convinced of his talent. He needed a patron, while she had long felt a void for the intellectual guidance and stimulation he was so willing to provide. It gave her a thrill to believe that her life was really worth something on an intellectual plane; apart from her thrilling and demanding work as a product tester, she was making her own small contribution to the furtherance of the Arts, through Herman, and she was not just another "dumb blonde" populating the world with nothing but babies. She knew that she *would* like to have a baby someday, but the values of her generation had taught her that having a baby was not really a *contribution* to anything; it was merely a biological whim that could be indulged if you so chose and could afford it, but you mustn't delude yourself into thinking of it as an *accomplishment* and you certainly must not have more than two.

The thing Cherry valued most in life was her relationship with Herman and the feeling it gave her that she was not just a sex object for men to jab their penises into. Herman was not like other men; he was more cultured, more refined. Thus he gave her respite from the attacks which were constantly launched against her by most men she encountered, who were single-mindedly bent on taking her to bed, to the point where a person with less pluck might just have stitched her vagina shut and joined a convent.

She sat on the couch next to Herman and placed her hand on his leg, causing him to tense a little. He rolled his eyes downward to stare at his shoes. Cherry put her arms around him, and a dreamy far-away look came over her. "We have so much to look forward to," she said wistfully. "Soon you'll be a successful writer. I'll quit my job and we'll get married. I can hardly wait!"

Herman grimaced. "You don't want to quit your job too soon," he admonished. "Lots of people quit their jobs and then they find out they can't get along without the money they were making. Marriages sometimes fall apart because of financial difficulties."

"We'll be all right," Cherry said brightly, "as long as we love each other." She hugged Herman tightly.

Squirming away from her and changing the subject, Herman said, "What are you testing tonight?"

"A new vibrator that clamps on a man's penis."

She got up from the couch, giving Herman a peck on his cheek, and went into the bathroom to pee and powder her nose. She flushed a little with the knowledge that she had lied to Herman, but she knew that the truth would have injured their relationship. She was not really going to test a new penis vibrator – she was going to meet up with Marcello Fettucini. He had stopped her in the hall after work to thank her for lying to Suck and to ask her to dinner. She thought it'd be all right to accept since, after all, he was quite harmless, with his 7.73 inch penis so mortifyingly inert.

But of course if he should miraculously recover tonight...

She would do the right thing in the line of duty and help make his recovery full and complete.

CHAPTER 11

At their table in an upscale Italian restaurant, Marcello smiled and clinked his champagne glass against Cherry's in a debonair manner, but in trying to propose a toast, he went all to pieces. "Here's to...uh...uh...to...uh...here's..."

"To us," Cherry concluded.

She sipped her champagne daintily while he downed his in a gulp and the bubbles went up his nose, sending him into a coughing fit. After he got himself under control, he said emphatically that he was not himself, and allowed his empty glass to come down onto the table so hard that the stem shattered and put a terrible gash in his hand. "Mama mia!" he exclaimed, and snatched up a dinner napkin and wrapped it around the injury, blood soaking into the white linen.

Cherry's lip trembled, but she could not think of anything to say.

"*Scusa*," Marcello said, and he got up and wandered through the crowded restaurant in search of a bandage, and by that time everyone was staring at him, but he did manage to get one from a cashier. When he sat back down across from Cherry, he seemed to have composed himself, and the waiter came and poured him a fresh glass of champagne. In his absence, the waiter had already cleared away the wreckage of the broken glass, and now he went away with the blood-soaked napkin.

Cherry resolutely managed not to stare at the few spots of blood that remained on the white tablecloth.

Marcello took a cautious sip of champagne, careful of the treacherous bubbles, and set his glass gently on the table, in front of his silverware. "I am-a sorry for my uncharacteristic clumsiness," he apologized. And then, after a pause, "Does-a your boyfriend know you are out-a with me?"

"I lied," Cherry admitted. "I don't know why. I told him I had to work overtime."

"You must-a tell him about...about my affliction, so he will not-a have-a to worry."

"Don't be so hard on...I mean, so difficult, with yourself," she said consolingly.

She set her glass down and began running her fingers around the rim; it was merely a nervous gesture but Marcello took it as a hint and leaned forward and poured her more champagne. Then, clearing his throat, he drew himself up and summoned the courage to say the things he knew he had to say. "You are so kind...so understanding. I felt-a I had-a to see you tonight to apologize for-a my failure earlier today...I...uh..."

She felt pity for him as his voice failed him and his eyes filled with tears.

"I have-a thought of killing myself," he announced sadly, then sank back, awed with the impact of what he had just spoken. He was overwhelmed with the unimaginable thought of a world made much more sorrowful because he would not be in it any longer.

A shudder went through Cherry and she fought not to start bawling. "No, don't you dare do it!" she blurted. "You're still *young*. Maybe they'll find a *cure*."

"I am like-a a bird without-a wings, a bull without horns," he said intensely.

51

"Like a bomb without a blast," Cherry added, in an attempt to show that she understood what he was driving at.

At that, the air went out of him and he began moaning softly with his head in his hands and everyone in the restaurant began staring at him again.

Cherry was a little flattered to be a central figure in such an intense drama. She felt honor-bound to try to help him and to save his life if possible. "Sex isn't everything," she said, even though she knew that she could not live without it. "You still have plenty to live for. Plays...good books."

"Bah!" Marcello said flatly.

"Herman says brainpower is what counts in today's world."

"You are truly fortunate. Herman sounds like-a a man who is secure inna his masculinity."

"He's wise beyond his years," Cherry affirmed.

"He is-a lucky to have-a you, Cherry. There will-a always be a warm-a place inna my heart for you." He took her hand in his and gazed deeply into her eyes, the way he had done with countless women in countless Italian restaurants in the good old days when his manhood was in full flower. But this time his lip trembled and he became morose and sullen.

The waiter brought their food, but he picked at his while Cherry ate voraciously and he envied her ability to eat like that and still remain svelte. He made a few attempts at clever conversation, which in the past had come so easily to him, but this time everything he said fell flat. Nevertheless Cherry seemed to enjoy his conversation. But his own heart was not in it.

CHAPTER 12

Herman had just finished putting on his Joyful Artificial breasts and was wriggling into a pair of Cherry's panties. It was Monday and the panties were embroidered *Tuesday* and Herman had tried to find the ones for Monday, but probably she was wearing them. They were not in the hamper. It was unlike her to wear panties when she knew she was going to work overtime and would just have to take them off. But Herman's mind did not dwell on this because he was so anxious for yet another erotic adventure.

He put on the pair labeled *Tuesday* and admired himself for a long time in the mirror while thrill after thrill coursed through him, until finally the sensations diminished and he decided to revive them by climbing into a pair of Cherry's pantyhose. But his perspiration made the hose stick to his skin and he had to struggle to get them on, and he punched a hole in them with his thumbnail, and before he could get them on all the way he had an orgasm. It was a tremendously fantastic orgasm, and he had to go to the bathroom to wash out Cherry's panties, and then he had to try to dry them quickly by blowing on them with her hairdryer, and this took up the remainder of the evening. As a result, Herman did not get any writing at all done that day, and he went to bed feeling guilty.

CHAPTER 13

Vernon Biggs had either to go to the hospital wearing a winter coat in the summertime, or carrying a cardboard box in front of himself. Or maybe he could pretend to have a heart attack, cover himself up with a blanket and let them take him to the emergency room in an ambulance.

He decided on the cardboard box and took a taxi.

The doctor was bright and diffident. "Penis under glass," he said, smiling. "Don't worry, I've seen this before. Amazing how many guys try it. You could have taken care of this yourself, you know."

And he smashed the orange juice bottle with a little metal mallet allowing the broken glass to fall into the wastebasket as Biggs's troublesome erection began to diminish. "The next time you do this," the doctor said, "you should use probably a milk bottle. Something larger, you see, that way you won't constrict the blood vessels."

Biggs put his penis in his pants and zipped his fly up, and the doctor handed him the cardboard box to take home, then said, "A milk bottle is not the best thing. I would prescribe that you try to find yourself a nice young lady."

"Thank you, Doctor," Biggs said. And he let himself out of the office, taking everything that had happened to heart and turning it all over in his mind, which was soon choked to the brim with unsavory lewd thoughts concerning Cherry Jankowski.

Unwittingly, the doctor's advice had put her in jeopardy. Her proximity to Vernon Biggs was her bad luck. But it is clear that the good doctor made a judgment error in not recommending a psychiatric examination for a young man who had entered the hospital with his penis stuck inside a bottle.

CHAPTER 14

Just as Mark Twain loved to write in bed, and Truman Capote loved to write in Holiday Inns, Herman had his own preference. He liked to write in drag. All of his best writing was done that way. It made him feel like Emily Dickinson, as though he had appropriated her muse. I bring this out because it is the sort of intimate detail that readers are fond of knowing about writers, and is exactly the kind of thing that would be probed and brought out in a colorful and delightful way, were Herman to be interviewed on PBS. He aspired that such an interview might take place someday, along with all the other trappings of acclaim and fame and glory, and he molded and developed his eccentricities accordingly. Writing in drag never failed to give him what he referred to as "an orgasm of the intellect." Colorful phrases and figures of speech gushed forth unrestrained. Onomatopoeia and hyperbole were effortless. Symbolism laced and threaded its way through his work. And, dressed as a woman, Herman always felt fully ready to give birth to poetic beauty. This particular method would probably not work well for every writer, but for Herman Longfellow it worked superbly well. It became his way of coping and surviving in a world that he recognized was more often than not hostile to genius and intolerant of the artistic temperament.

CHAPTER 15

Sick in both body and spirit, Marcello went to the home of his parents for Sunday dinner. On the phone Mama Fettucini had broken into tears and insisted that he come. (Her Italian accent was more pronounced than his, so I will try to duplicate it here, in print.) She said, "You mama is-a still you mama. Nonchou fo'get that. If-a you have trouble you come-a to see you mama, she never turn-a you away."

Marcello's mother, dad and brother knew about his affliction and they were trying to cope with it, although the humiliation and disgrace were almost unbearable. They could not understand how such a thing could happen to *any* Italian, much less a Fettucini, whose men folk had been notorious even in the Old Country for their hot blood and perpetual erections.

When Marcello entered the house, his mama kissed him and tried unsuccessfully to restrain her tears. His papa did not look up from the table but muttered Italian curse words under his breath. His brother Angelo scowled and hitched up his shoulder holster to relieve the sore spot his heavy .45 caliber automatic was making under his armpit. Although the family never talked about it or admitted it openly, even to themselves, they all knew with a suspicion just shy of certainty that Angie was a member of the Black Hand. Sometimes he stayed in the house for months, pacing and peeking out anxiously between the slats of the Venetian blinds; and at other times he stayed in his room for long hours, soaking .45 caliber bullets in rotten garlic to make them poisonous – and then finally one dark evening he would go out, and the next morning's newspaper would carry headlines concerning a mobster gunned down in an alley or garroted in a parking lot or decapitated in a barber shop or nailed with ten-penny nails through his hands and feet to the dirty floor of an abandoned warehouse, his gonads stuffed in his mouth as a warning that stoolpigeons ought to keep their mouths shut.

Marcello sat down at the big kitchen table and Mama shoved a big plate of spaghetti and meatballs in front of him while Papa, glowering savagely, stabbed a fork into one of his own meatballs and swallowed it whole, the sauce running down his lips like blood. He stuffed down half a slice of Italian bread as wadding after the meatball, and the look on his face conveyed the impression that he would have preferred to bite off somebody's head.

Papa's anger had Marcello so shook up that he lost his appetite, if he ever had any. His shoulders slumped as Mama put one of her fat arms around him and said, "*Mangia*, Marcello, *mangia*! You no look-a too good. Too skinny. *Mangia*! Getta back-a you strength!"

"Mama, I..I already weigh two hundred and-a twenty pounds."

Angie snickered suddenly, Papa snorted, and Marcello hung his head.

Mama made the Sign of the Cross and waved her sauce-stained ladle in Marcello's face. Sternly and shrilly, she lectured him. "You should-a go to church! You used-a to be altar boy! I was-a so proud! Look-a you brother Angie – *he* goes-a to church and he gotta lots of-a pretty gal!"

Angie snickered again.

Papa swallowed a stuffed olive in one gulp and glowered at Marcello, who flinched, half expecting a clout to the ear.

Mama's eyes watered as they fell on the Crucifix hanging on the wall. "I pray every night-a for you, Marcello! I'm-a pray to the Blessed Virgin! I ask-a her to help you so you no lose-a you job. Look-a you brother Angie – *he* gotta a *good-a* job. He gotta big-a car, and lotsa money inna the mattress up stairs."

Defensively, Marcello shot back, "If he had-a a decent job he wouldn't have-a to hide his money inna a mattress."

A stunned silence filled the room.

Mama nervously wiped her hands on her apron and looked toward the front door as if the cops might burst in.

Papa gulped down another olive.

Angie whistled through his teeth, very softly and ominously. The he laughed maliciously, threateningly, till the laugh sweetened itself gradually, slowly freeing itself of malice. When the laugh died away, Angie leaned forward and hitched up his shoulder holster and stabbed his fork into a meatball.

The room came to life again.

Mama's eyes came to rest on her prized painting of the Bleeding Heart of Jesus, on the wall opposite the Crucifix, and she remembered how she had carefully wrapped the Crucifix and the Bleeding Heart in a blanket to bring them all the way to America by boat with her and Papa, and again she blessed herself with the Sign of the Cross. "You should-a go to church," she said again to Marcello. "Talk-a to the priest. You papa never hadda no trouble like-a you have. Maybe Papa canna teach-a you whatta to do."

At this, Papa jumped up, slammed both fists on the table, making his silverware pop into the air come down with a loud clatter, and roared, "He's-a *notta* my son!"

"You shutta uppa you face!" Mama yelled, and with a menacing gesture she threatened to clout Papa with her sauce-stained ladle.

Papa angrily swiped his napkin across his face and said, "*Angie* is-a my son! He knows-a whatta he got between his-a legs! Marcello is-a notta my son. He make-a me shame."

Mama began to cry. "You no talk-a like-a that, Papa. It's a *sin*! Marcello is-a a good-a boy. When he getta well again, he gonna make-a you proud."

Tearfully, Mama kissed her eldest son on the cheek. But Papa was unmoved. Marcello saw that he must say something to prevent the family from falling apart. "Please," he pleaded with them all. "Please, do notta fight because of-a me. Whatever is-a wrong with-a me, I do notta understand. But I will disgrace-a the *familia* no longer. I will stay away until I canna be myself again. Goodbye, Mama...and Papa. Goodbye, Angie. I ask-a you to pray for me. You will notta see me again until I am a well man."

Marcello rose to his feet with as much dignity as he could muster. He kissed Mama on her forehead, offered his hand to Papa, which was turned down, shrugged helplessly toward Angie, and as they all stared after him with mixed emotions, he shuffled sadly across the living room and went out the door.

Angie scowled and lit up a cigarette. Then, hitching up his shoulder holster, he got up from the kitchen table and went upstairs to be alone in his room. But even through the closed door he could still hear Mama's sobs, and he did not like to hear Mama cry. He reached the decision that, for Mama's sake and for the sake of the family, he had to do something to help his older brother.

CHAPTER 16

Marcello considered going to Confession. But today was Sunday. The church did not have regular Confession hours on Sunday, so if he wanted to confess he'd have to go to the rectory and knock on the door and ask to see the priest. He did not care for the prospect of confronting the priest or even maybe the cleaning lady face to face, so he decided to simply go to the church and say a prayer.

He walked several blocks, hoping the exercise might help his affliction in some tiny way, and arrived in front of the little Roman Catholic church where in his teen years he had been an altar boy and had worried about masturbating and going to hell, and later had worried about having sexual intercourse with a pretty little choir girl who always cried while they were doing it because she had wanted to become a nun, until he had heard the priest fart one day while genuflecting during mass, and somehow the revelation that the priest had to fart like everybody else had shaken Marcello's belief in the sacredness of anything, and he found himself an agnostic at a tender age while all his friends were still memorizing catechism.

As he approached the steps of the church, an old lady dressed entirely in black hobbled out on crutches, and he held the heavy doors open for her as he went in. He dipped his fingers in oily Holy Water and blessed himself as the stale odors of the church wafted over him. He knelt and prayed, searching for the right words and making them come out, all the while wondering if it was right to pray for his sort of problem, and finally reasoning that not being able to propitiate the race of man as God had commanded was probably much more upsetting to the Divine Plan than getting the measles or the sore throat, and nobody had ever said that it was wrong to pray to get better from the measles or the sore throat. Nevertheless the prayer did not make him feel any better, and with some misgivings he left the church and went to see his old girlfriend, Angela, the ex-choir girl of his youth, who had always been more effective than prayer when it came to getting him an erection.

He walked to her place, not far from the church, and when he rang the bell she flung the door wide and was wearing nothing but a filmy nightgown. "Marcello!" she exclaimed, smiling and very glad to see him. She was still quite beautiful, darkly tanned and just slightly plump, and at the moment he could not recall any good reason why they had drifted apart. After all, he had been fully able to perform way back then.

"Angela," he moaned, his voice laden with remorse and agony.

"What a surprise! Come on in. Don't just stand there. You look so sad."

He followed her to a seat on the couch. But he could not find any words to say until she reached out tenderly and touched his cheek. "Angela...I must-a tell you...I am impotent." Her eyes widened with disbelief. When she tentatively put her hand on his crotch, he recoiled. "It's true," he said miserably. "You have notta heard?"

"No, not a word. I don't get downtown much anymore."

She unzipped his fly and pulled out his shriveled penis and looked at it quizzically, remembering its wonderful past performances, then bent it back and forth in her hand, examining it the way you might examine a child suspected of not washing behind his ears. "It looks healthy enough," she pronounced finally, but Marcello squirmed uncomfortably and cast his eyes toward the ceiling.

"I bet we can make him his old self again," Angela said, smiling. And when she bent toward his loins and took his limp penis into her mouth, it was difficult for him to believe that she had once wanted to become a nun. He reached for her and fondled her firm, ample breasts, and realized she must have had implants. "Please, it's-a no use," he murmured, as out of habit he rubbed her hard nipples against his palms.

At that moment there was a noise on the stairs, and a man entered the room – and Marcello jumped up so fast that Angela's teeth scraped his penis as it popped out of her mouth, and he let out a scream and began hopping around the room in a doubled-up position, which only added to his feelings of embarrassment and humiliation. The strange man, who was totally nude, looked on calmly, with shaving cream smeared on one half of his face.

"Marcello, this is my husband, Fred," Angela explained, after Marcello had partially calmed down. And Fred warmly said, "How do you do?"

Marcello collapsed heavily onto the couch and zipped up his fly. "*Scusa – scusa*, please," was all he could muster by way of apology, and he half expected Fred to draw a gun and shoot him, even though Fred certainly could not be concealing a weapon on his person and did not seem to be making a move to get one. So Marcello relaxed a little.

Fred sat down and patted Marcello on the back. "You don't have to apologize. Really, it's okay. Angela and I aren't old-fashioned."

Angela unzipped Marcello's fly again and fondled his penis, checking where her teeth had scraped it and saying, "It appears all right." Fred wiped shaving cream from his face and looked on with considerable interest. "We're swingers," Angela explained. "So are all our friends. It's the greatest!"

"Besides, we're AC-DC," Fred added with a friendly smile, as he put his hand on Marcello's leg and leaned forward to examine the soft but large penis in his wife's hand.

Marcello gulped and became uncomfortable. Truth is, he was somewhat of a homophobe, even in this enlightened period of American history. Angela resumed sucking his penis but because of his mixed feelings it was not arousing him, and Fred sensed this, and he became sympathetic and reassuring, saying, "Listen, I couldn't help overhearing. You're having a problem that's got you upset."

"Yes, terrible," Marcello admitted. "Terrible. It-a never happened before-a to me."

"It happened to me once," Fred said, unashamed. "It made me feel so low I couldn't stand it. You're working too hard, that's all."

"I'm notta working at all," Marcello said hopelessly. And Angela, undaunted, continued to suck his penis, trying to impress him with how much she had improved since the days when they used to make love in the quoir loft.

"Look, I have a tremendous idea," Fred said. When I was having your problem, I went to a party. An orgy, a real turn -on. Why don't you watch me and Angela?"

"That sounds fantabulous!" Angela said.

Soon both she and Fred were nude and getting into a 69 position.

"Just watch Angela and me," Fred mumbled against his wife's flesh. "When you get turned on, just join in."

"Would you care for a glass of wine or something while you watch?" Angela said. "I'm sorry, I should've asked sooner."

"No...uh...go ahead...enjoy yourselves," Marcello told them.

To his consternation, his penis was shriveling even more, instead of growing larger, and he felt an uncontrollable urge to get out of there. To be by himself somewhere, away from the good intentions of others.

When Fred and Angela were so immersed in what they were doing that they weren't paying much attention to him, Marcello tiptoed past them and went out the door. They never even noticed, moaning, heaving and thrashing with their first orgasm of this brand new session, and when they relaxed and lit up cigarettes, Fred said, "I just realized your pal Marcello is gone."

"Maybe we should've offered him something to eat," Angela wondered out loud.

"We were more than kind to him," Fred told her. "Maybe he *is* some kind of pervert."

"He's nothing like he used to be, I can tell you that," Angela said, wistfully reminiscing.

She tried to pull Fred into her arms for another interlude, but he said, "Naw, there's no audience now. I can't get into it so much."

He pushed Angela away and got up to look for the remote. It was almost time for a movie he wanted to watch, a mobster flick full of blood and violence.

CHAPTER 17

On late Sunday afternoon, the Theophilus Suck family sunbathed in the nude together in the privacy of their suburban backyard. Evangeline Suck, deeply engrossed in a book entitled *Incest: The New Permissiveness*, groped for her lemonade and inadvertently stuck her fingers in it, nearly upsetting the glass. She licked her fingers painstakingly clean so they wouldn't get her book sticky, and glanced over at Theophilus, who reminded her of a corpse the way he was sprawled out in his webbed lawn chair, and at their son Abraham, bald, 21 years old and severely retarded, who was playing with his toy dump truck, running it back and forth in a patch of yellow clay in the center of the lawn.

Evangeline's voice rang out, fraught with the concern of a mother for the wellbeing of her offspring. "Abraham! Don't kneel in the dirt, Abraham!"

She had noticed that Abraham's penis was dangling almost low enough to touch the ground as he knelt there in the patch of yellow clay, and she feared that the urethra might become clogged and infected, although she had never read of a case history or heard any rumors about such a thing, and deep down inside she had to admit to herself that yelling a warning to Abraham (poor dull-headed child) was as futile as banging a gong when the moon was about to be struck by a meteor.

As luck would have it, of his own volition Abraham sat back in the grass in such a way that the blades of grass tickling the head of his penis would have given a normal boy an erection, and Evangeline breathed a sigh of relief that her son was out of danger, except there was still the very viable possibility that a bumblebee lurking in the grass might sting him on his scrotum. Because Theophilus had told her of how erection failures among male product testers in the Joyful labs were quite bad for business, she wondered if bee or hornet stings might somehow be employed to make male organs swell artificially, but then, how would the engineers deal with the pain? Perhaps a topical analgesic would do.

She had an active and inquisitive mind that she was very proud of, and so she was always open to new ways of thinking and dealing with sticky problems. Accordingly, as her eyes fastened upon the tufts of coarse black hair on Abraham's back, her mind wandered away from reading about fathers and mothers and brothers and sisters having sex with their fathers and mothers and brothers and sisters in her book called *Incest: The New Permissiveness* and she thought what a lousy shame it was that she could not just extract the ugly useless hair on Abraham's back and use it to patch the bald spot on his head. She had an obsession with making the boy look as young as possible, in the hopes that if he *looked* young people might not expect too much from him in the way of adeptness or astuteness. Evangeline, remember, was a creature of her time, and had not been exposed to enlightened ways of thinking about folks with mental insufficiencies, and so her attitudes to even her own son were quite crude by standards that evolved later in the *zeitgeist* of our society.

Theophilus grunted and sat up, struggling, because of his bloated paunch and weak abdominal muscles, and Evangeline looked over and fleetingly scrutinized his penis. It was flaccid and shriveled below the level of response-readiness in a healthy, active penis, and a piece of lint and a couple of wiry public hairs were sticking out from under the foreskin, and Evangeline could not help the contempt she felt for her husband at the realization that a more conscientious man would have skinned it back and removed the lint and hairs just out of pride and self-respect. Her disdain was aggravated by the fact that, lately, his sexual efforts had reduced themselves to bringing home a new dildo or vibrator now and then from the factory, the way some men bring home a box of candy or a dozen roses.

"I'm going in the house," Theophilus said, and he glanced down at his penis but did not bother to remove the lint or the hairs.

"Lie back down, dear," his wife told him. "You need some sun, you're white as a fish belly. The Vitamin D is good for the pimples on your back."

"No," Theophilus said. "It's too hot out here. I feel weak. I'm going inside to soak in the bathtub."

He got to his feet, and she watched his flabby buttocks shaking like a bowl full of jelly as he trudged toward the house and let himself in through the basement. The screen door slammed shut as Evangeline found her place in *Incest: The New Permissiveness* wherein the author, a world-renowned psychiatrist named Dr. Julius Stuttgart, summed up the chapter she was reading as follows:

Therefore Sarah and Ben, though mother and son, found that they could please each other in ways that far exceeded the pleasure that had been their lot in a more conventional parent-offspring arrangement. This stripped them of their inhibitions and revealed their deepest needs, one to another. Thus Ben was able to relate to his mother as a person, not merely a symbol of authority. And Sarah, for her part, found an outlet for the filial attraction she felt for her son, whereas in a conventional relationship these feelings are inhibited and denied. Besides, in these days of error-free birth control, they both knew that they need have no fear of the sort that iron-age peoples used to have, of producing a hemophiliac or a hair lip.

As Evangeline read on, deeply moved by the truth and lucidity of what Dr. Julius Stuttgart was saying, Abraham had begun to carefully, methodically, rip up the flowers at the edge of the lawn. She had painstakingly planted those flowers and had labored over them daily with the loving attention so vital to their successful cultivation. Now Abraham was tending to their destruction, with a dumb but intense look on his cherubic face. And, unknown to Evangeline, to him what he was doing had a purpose and a logic. You see, he had gleaned a cursory knowledge of the workings of trucks from watching a construction project near the house, and he loved to play for hours with the red toy dump truck his father had bought for him, and he did not understand anything about flowers and the special exemption from destruction granted them by most people along with a vast measure of esteem and affection. As far as he was concerned, the white petals from the flowers marked the places where the truck had to pick up workers or let them off, and the heads of the flowers with their big yellow centers were in a pile and they had to be picked up and carried to the other side of the yellow clay to be dumped on the edge of the grass.

If Evangeline had known that Abraham had figured out all of this for himself, she would have been thrilled and proud. But she did not know, and when she came up behind Abraham and yelled at him, he was nonplussed. Or he would have been, except he didn't hear her. He just sat there with a flower in his hand and his penis dangling in the dirt, and when his mother started hitting him with her book, he started to cry.

"Up to your bedroom! Up to your bedroom!" Evangeline started to yell, and it made quite a scene to see this nude, bald, 21-year-old man struggling with his naked mother for possession of a red toy dump truck while she kept beating him on his rump with a book entitled *Incest: The New Permissiveness.*

Finally she stopped hitting him, and Abraham backed sheepishly away from her.

"Give me that dump truck!" Evangeline said sternly, and Abraham forked it over. Then she resumed beating him with her book on his pimpled backside, as she led him upstairs to his bedroom and shoved him inside and locked the door. And she was so angry that she did not notice that her spanking had squashed some of his pimples, and they were oozing. He did not notice this either.

He rolled over and lay still, with his hands folded across his belly. The toy dump truck popped momentarily into his mind, just the image of it with no other associations or plans, and then the image faded.

Where his hand were cupped over his groin, his belly felt warm and tickly, and he took his hands away and looked at the dirt on them, then returned them to the warm and tickly place. He lowered his right hand to where it felt warm and jittery and good. He rubbed and touched it all over, and he looked at it and it kept feeling better, and he began rubbing harder and harder, and the good tingly feeling got stronger and stronger until he couldn't stand it and it felt better than anything he had ever felt, and he almost got dizzy and he couldn't get his breath when the whole room seemed to spin and good feelings shot through him in a big way, and then he just lay there on his back feeling weak and funny, like someone had just stopped tickling him.

Suddenly he saw his mother standing in the doorway.

"Well, it appears you've discovered something new, dear," she said, smiling.

And sad to say, some sick thoughts came into her mind, inspired by the book *Incest: The New permissiveness* by Dr. Julius Stuttgart. It goes to show the adverse effect that perverse scientists like Stuttgart have on society when they dignify wanton, immoral concepts between covers, thereby warping the minds of impressionable people who believe that seeing a thing in print sanctifies it, and who would be decent, proper citizens if they never had to look at or read anything lewd or perverse.

Not that I'm in favor of censorship.

Freedom of speech is essential for scholarly works such as mine. That much is certainly true.

We can't let the rotten apples spoil the whole barrel.

I interviewed Evangeline during the writing of this book, and she was quite coy with me over the subject of whether or not anything untoward had ever transpired between her and her son Abraham.

CHAPTER 18

The doorbell rang and Cherry wiped toothpaste from her mouth and went to answer it. When she opened the door, she was confronted by Vernon Biggs, who gave her a syrupy smile and ran his lecherous eyes up and down her body. She happened to be wearing a football jersey with a number 69 on it.

"Would you mind terribly if I asked you to give me a hand with something?" Biggs asked.

Cherry was a little leery of Biggs because he was always waving his penis at her.

"My new drapes," Biggs said. "They were delivered last evening, and I'm having Mother over to supper today."

Cherry thought maybe he was a nicer guy than she had thought since he was being so nice to his mother, so she smiled and said, "Sure, no problem." She imagined that maybe if she were nice to Biggs he'd mellow reciprocally and stop waving his penis at her. She wasn't terribly impressed by it anyhow. It was only about five inches long.

"I don't mean to impose on you," he said, as they entered his apartment and he closed the door and slid the bolt shut.

Cherry innocently looked around. There was indeed a stepladder piled with drapes, in front of a very large bare window.

"I'm embarrassed to tell you this," Biggs said. "I have a touch of vertigo, from the war."

"Vertigo?" Cherry mumbled, thinking it was such a funny, incomprehensible word.

"I get dizzy," Biggs explained, trying not to show how exasperated he was by her ignorance. Here he was, working hard to make up a phony but clever story, and she was so dumb she didn't appreciate it. But he went on. "My chopper was shot down by some crazy gooks and I barely survived. My mind is laced with memories of spinning and plummeting toward the earth. I can't even talk about it anymore. I'm afraid of high places."

"Oh...I'm sorry," Cherry said. And she felt guilty because she was a woman and never had to go into combat.

"Maybe you should go up on the ladder and I can hand you the drapes," Biggs suggested.

Cherry glanced at him sympathetically and began climbing the ladder, offering Biggs a wonderfully explicit view of luscious legs and bare bottom because underneath the football jersey she was wearing nothing at all. Unknown to the innocent girl, Biggs already had an erection lurking under the flaps of his plaid bathrobe, and his lusts got fired to a fever pitch by watching her go up the ladder. The malarkey about the drapes and the vertigo was part of a nefarious plan that had been developing in Biggs's mind as a result of his discomforting episode with the juice bottle and the resultant well-meaning advice from the kindly doctor who broke the bottle with his hammer.

In a twinkling, while Cherry was trying to help him hang his drapes, his arms shot out and seized her around her waist and tackled her to the floor. She was no match for him. And he shoved his medium-sized penis straight in her.

The doctor was right, Biggs immediately realized. It felt better than a glass bottle. And although he didn't know it and could not have cared, she was spared physical pain which would have accompanied her mental anguish over what he was doing to her, because she had applied petroleum jelly in preparation for her work that day at Joyful Novelties.

Smarting from embarrassment and humiliation, she gasped and yelled for Herman once or twice, but gave it up when he failed to come to her rescue. Hating herself for it, but powerless to prevent the natural workings of her own body, Cherry climaxed along with Biggs and then allowed herself to be half-pushed, half escorted, out into the hall, where Biggs slammed his door on her, and she began to cry.

Let me tell you in no uncertain terms that I absolutely do not condone what just happened. I despise rapists and men who exploit women in lesser ways that still cause women pain. I do not know why some women fall so hard for the so-called "bad boys." I think it's because these women have an innate sense that mean and rough fellows will be their best protectors. And then these dirty rascals that they hook up with proceed to victimize and abuse them – and often kill them.

What did Biggs care about such matters? He was in it for his own gratification. Having gotten his way, he wrapped his drooping penis in a soft tissue so it would not drip on his way across the carpet, and went into the bathroom to soak in the tub; he had thoughtfully prepared it beforehand with aromatic bath oil and lots of warm, soapy bubbles. The dreamy satisfaction that a normal man feels after sexual intercourse washed over him, even though he had nothing to be proud of and did not admit it. He began to hum softly to himself as he soaped his body.

Meantime, in her own bathroom, behind the locked door, Cherry dried her tears and washed herself up and began to get dressed for work. She resolved not to upset Herman by telling him about the incident with Biggs. But her heart was broken, and she couldn't help feeling bad about her decadent neighbor and the sordid experience he had forced on her.

Soon she came to believe it was probably her own fault: a reaction in females that sordid persons such as Biggs fervently hope for and are so adept at implanting and encouraging. They know that women innately, in evolutionary terms, have an ingrained fear of losing approval and thus losing a spouse, a protector or an illicit sexual partner, and so females of our species are very susceptible to blaming themselves for whatever happens to them, even though they may not be truly responsible in the least. Despicable persons such as Vernon Biggs know exactly how to manipulate such women and how to utilize their self-doubts and their tendency toward guilt complexes to an unscrupulous male's advantage.

Now that he had used his nefarious talents on Cherry, the poor thing was actually thinking that maybe she needed to see a psychiatrist. But for the time being, she put off making an appointment. Herman wouldn't want her to spend the money.

CHAPTER 19

In a noisy shower room at Joyful Novelties, Inc., Marcello Fettucini was enduring another brow-beating from Theophilus Suck. Marcello was nude, his body dripping-wet from the shower, while Suck was in street clothes. Male and female product testers still in the showers were laughing and tossing bars of soap around and cracking dirty jokes, while Suck yelled at Marcello, not sparing the younger man's feelings.

"What's wrong with you, you pathetic so-and-so? Can you give me a clue? A hint? A reason to believe in you so I won't have to fire you?"

"I do not-a know," Marcello admitted apologetically.

"Ten erection failures in one week!" Suck exclaimed.

"Seven," Marcello corrected. "Seven this-a week and three last-a week. Ten inna fourteen days." He was anxious to make the statistics look as favorable as possible.

"Every time there's an erection failure it costs this company money," Suck pointed out for the umpteenth time.

"I do not-a know what-a else I can do," Marcello pleaded. "I eat-a yogurt. I take-a Vitamin E."

"You're gonna have to pull yourself up by your boot straps," Suck said. "Good jobs are hard to find. You foreigners are all alike, you expect to find our streets paved with gold. I have a board of directors meeting later this month and I won't be able to hide the facts from them any longer."

Suck turned and walked slowly away with his hands clasped behind his back like a man with the weight of the world upon his shoulders. Marcello watched him go, then started toweling himself off. His face was red from embarrassment, and he was in a hurry to get out of the locker room. A gang of male and female product testers still under the showers began laughing at him and singing *You're an old softie* to the tune *of You're an old smoothie* while they splashed in the water and tossed a bar of soap back and forth.

Marcello could not help feeling totally humiliated.

Suicidal thoughts were very strong in his mind as he rubbed his penis and testicles dry very carefully, as though he feared to touch them.

CHAPTER 20

That very evening there was an attempt made on Suck's life which was not recognized by him as anything more than a harmless practical joke, and so he neglected to report it to the police. The fact that there had been an attempted murder went entirely unsuspected. What happened was this:

Someone sneaked into Suck's bedroom late at night through an opened window, spied a form lying under the bed covers, crept stealthily to the edge of the bed and plunged a 14-inch knife into the sleeping form. Doubtless the unknown villain was startled by the resulting explosion, as the form under the covers was only Suck's inflatable Party Doll, which he had taken to using on occasion, like a teddy bear.

In any event, the villain fled, and when Suck stepped out of the bathroom with his trousers half down and a sheet of toilet paper in his hand, he discovered only the mutilated and deflated Joyful Party Doll and the 14-inch knife.

Since he had no reason to suspect that he would have any personal enemies – after all, he was a benefactor to all of mankind – Theophilus persuaded himself to dismiss the bizarre occurrence and to believe that it would probably not happen again.

CHAPTER 21

On a Saturday afternoon, Stag the janitor's artificial vagina arrived in the mail in a plain brown wrapper, but when he tried to use it he found that it was too small. Highly disappointed, he had to re-wrap it and send it back for another.

Along with it had come a free deck of playing cards, a pinochle deck, with pictures on the backs of the cards of people fornicating and performing fellatio and cunnilingus, and although Stag considered oral sex to be depraved and un-American, the cards showing fellatio and cunnilingus were the ones he looked at while he masturbated in lieu of using his artificial vagina after he had found it was too small for him and had sent it back to the factory.

Stag's disappointment was a personal, emotional thing which almost ruined his day for him, yet the return of the artificial vagina was not in any way traumatic at Joyful and it was merely listed on the ledgers as one more item in the register of callbacks and exchanges, which impeded the company's profits and efficiency but were not usually dealt with in any flustered way, except the workers on the production line were being constantly exhorted to use stricter product control in an effort to reduce callbacks and exchanges.

This is a sad state of affairs and goes to show how modern factories have come largely to disregard the human element. In days past, when a man bought a suit he went to a tailor whom he had probably known all his life and got measured up for the new suit, and talked with his friend the

79

tailor about the government and the neighbors and the rainfall and the crops. And he probably knew the tailor's wife and kids, and he got maybe a cup of coffee and a piece of apple cobbler when he came to pick the suit up and take it home with him. And the suit usually fit properly, too and the stitches did not come apart at the seams even after it was handed down two or three generations.

It is striking how our modern factories churn out millions of products for human consumption without needing to involve themselves in any human contact whatsoever with the ultimate consumers of the products. It produces disappointments such as the one Stag felt when he received an artificial vagina which was too small for him, after he had built his hopes up and was in a fever to use it and enjoy its benefits – benefits which had been extolled by means of lavish advertising which had caused Stag to save up his good money and spend it for a product which did not meet his expectations.

American industry thus throws itself open to criticism. And it can easily be seen why there has been such a decline in our Gross National Product. We cannot continue to be a great trading nation if we cannot turn out goods of consistent high quality, and it is long past time for us to re-examine and re-evaluate our ideals and our methods.

CHAPTER 22

The Joyful engineer held in his hand a tiny whirring vibrator designed to clamp around the base of a man's penis, while Cherry and the Male Tester stood by, in the nude, awaiting their instructions.

"This device provides super-ordinary stimulation to both penis and vagina during intercourse," the Chief Engineer said. "It will aid in rendering a super-ordinary climax to both male and female. The only question is, can the male withstand the additional stimulation without climaxing too soon, thus spoiling it for his partner?"

Cherry and the Male Tester sat on the edge of the testing lab bed while the aides and engineers checked and adjusted their equipment and tinkered with dials and switches. As a matter of habit, Cherry took the Male Tester's penis in her hand and massaged it deftly, and the Chief Engineer admonished, "Be careful not to get him too excited beforehand because it will ruin the test. As soon as he acquires an erection he has to put this on." He handed the tiny vibrating device to the Male Tester.

"We want to see if he can give you a climax without ejaculating too soon," an Assistant Engineer elucidated.

"That's correct," the Chief Engineer agreed. "We know this is going to be a popular item with the ladies, but it's no good if it stimulates the man too much."

"Premature ejaculation is already quite a pernicious problem in America," the Assistant Engineer reminded.

"I see," Cherry said, proud to demonstrate her cognitive intelligence. "You want us to do it straight. Conservative."

81

Here in the testing lab, she was completely at ease and self-confident – because she knew exactly what her job was, and she knew she could do it better than most of the other female testers. Whatever guilt feelings might have bothered her initially, when she first took the job, had melted away in the ego-glow and warm pride that comes with finding a niche in the world, a niche that provides a much needed sense of accomplishment.

The Male Tester now had a good, strong erection, and he clamped the vibrator onto his penis. So one of the aides pressed a button that caused the bed to rise pneumatically to the proper height for scientific observation, as Cherry spread her legs wide and helped the Male Tester with his insertion.

"Let us know when each of you reach climax," one of the assistants said. "That's an important part of the data."

But Cherry barely heard him. Already the vibrating penis, with its rhythmic plunges and thrusts, was driving her toward a frenzied orgasm.

The Male Tester was whimpering and moaning as he drove his penis in and out of her, while striving mightily at the same time to withhold his ejaculation. He felt as though his load of semen was being drawn up out of his testicles with a force that was overpoweringly explosive. To draw his mind away from this effect, he tried to imagine himself being crucified. It helped a little bit. He lay back and did not move, for perhaps one or two heartbeats. Then he drove deeply into her.

She began writhing and screaming. Herman's face came into her mind but was driven out by the sheer overpowering shudder of delight created by the plunging, vibrating penis deep inside her.

The video crew moved in closer. For the first time in weeks, the director ordered a facial close-up – something that was usually overlooked in favor of tight shots of gonads, labia and wet, thrusting phalluses. There was an extraordinarily tortured, yet beautiful and unworldly look on Cherry's lovely countenance. "Uh! Oh! I'm coming! I'm coming...I'm COMING!" she cried out as she heaved and thrashed wildly – and one of the aides bent over her with his stopwatch. "Three minutes, thirty-five seconds," the aide said.

The Chief Engineer flipped through a sheaf of papers on his clipboard. "Let's see...oh, yes...very good. Your average climax under normal intercourse takes five minutes, thirty-nine seconds. The penis vibrator definitely accelerates climax."

"I came, too," the Male Tester said weakly. And all the engineers and aides stared at him as they realized it was the first time he had been able to articulate his experience.

"We got the results we expected," the Chief Engineer said. "How do you feel?"

"Fine. Great. It was a fantastic climax. Impossible to hold back, though." He sounded terribly spent, and was making no effort to roll out from between Cherry's legs.

"Do you think you could go again?" the Chief Engineer asked.

"Yes...in a little while. Maybe with a little help."

"Help him, Cherry," the Chief Engineer instructed.

"How?" she asked innocently.

"Use your imagination. Turn the vibrator back on. This time we're interested in the amount of time it takes you to get ready, as well as the amount of time to your second orgasm. We will discuss quality of orgasm in the critique session to follow."

Cherry concentrated hard on what the Chief Engineer was telling her, as the vibrator was back on again, making its whirring electrical sound, and the Male Tester's penis was beginning to stiffen and enlarge inside her vagina.

The engineers and assistants were probing around, taking notes and examining gauges and dials.

Dimly, in the rear of the lab somewhere, Cherry could hear someone laughing. Just a laugh. Disembodied. With no explanation to it.

CHAPTER 23

Miss Cornelia Peabody, assistant and receptionist to Dr. Julius Stuttgart, psychiatrist, typed Cherry's initial data onto a three-by-five card.

JANKOWSKI, CHERRY
AGE: 19
SEX: FEMALE
SUFFERS FROM EROTIC FANTASIES
AND EROTIC DELUSIONS.

Then Miss Peabody looked up from her typewriter and allowed her mouth to form itself into the sort of professional smile that is always to be found on those professionals who habitually distance themselves from any deep interest in their clients. In an impersonal tone, she said, "Go right in, Miss Jankowski. Dr. Stuttgart will be with you in a moment."

Cherry stepped into an office adjacent to the reception area, where there was an old-fashioned psychiatrist's couch, a bicycle exerciser, and a toucan in a large, smelly cage. There was also a set of book shelves filled entirely with copies of just one book, *Incest: The New Permissiveness*, by Dr. Julius Stuttgart. Cherry was impressed by the intellectual sound of the book's title and its leather binding, which reminded her of the *Encyclopedia Brittanica.*

She sat on the couch and began nervously re-applying her lipstick.

The toucan was hanging by its claws onto one side of its wire cage, and was tugging with its horny curved beak at a sliding wire door which, if it could be lifted all the way up, would give the bird its freedom; but every time the bird got the door halfway up it slid shut again, because the dumb creature failed to realize it could hold the door partially open with its head and then use its claws to slide it up the rest of the way. This action by the toucan of getting the door partly open only to have it slide shut again happened about twenty-five times while Cherry sat there wondering and worrying about how dangerous the bird might be if it got loose; i.e., maybe it would fly at her and claw her eyes out. She wondered why a psychiatrist needed a bird like that and why all the heavy drapes in the office were drawn tightly shut even though it was bright and sunny outside. She did not know, by the way, that the bird was called a toucan; to her, it was just some kind of dyed parrot. But she did figure out after a while that it was probably too dumb to realize how to escape by lifting the wire door.

Eventually Dr. Julius Stuttgart, world-renowned psychiatrist, made his appearance. He lingered just inside the doorway while he helped himself to a cup of water from the water cooler. Then he smiled at Cherry and rubbed the palms of his hands together in anticipation of their encounter. She noticed that he had a large brown stain on the front of his white shirt, and it looked like a coffee stain. He had a beard and mustache and a monocle, which helped to fulfill Cherry's preconceptions of what a psychiatrist should look like and also went a long way toward enlisting her complete confidence.

"Miss Jankowski!" the good doctor exclaimed with unbridled enthusiasm as he looked her over.

"Yes, Doctor Stuttgart?"

Stuttgart did not reply. Instead he paused by the bird cage, grinned maliciously at the toucan, and slammed the wire door shut on its claws, then used a sharp pencil to poke the bird toward the rear of its cage. After he completed this bit of business, he seemed satisfied, and Cherry tried to think that maybe that was the way parrots had to be trained. She was also quite relieved that the danger of the bird's escaping had been at least temporarily aborted. Not that she didn't feel sorry for the bird. She did. But her own safety seemed of primary importance.

She looked quizzically up at Stuttgart as he advanced toward her and paused at the foot of the couch. He said, "Lie down, won't you please? Yes...yes...that's better. Much more comfortable...now we can talk."

He got to his knees in front of the couch, which was something Cherry was not prepared for but she was even less prepared for what he did next. That is, he spread her legs wide apart, hiked up her skirt, and allowed his right hand to rest on her crotch. She jumped up, startled, and exclaimed, "Doctor!"

"God, you frightened me!" Stuttgart said, clutching his hand to his breast. "Your nerves must be shot, my dear. You nearly scared me out of my wits. I was merely testing your responses, my dear. These physical things sometimes have a direct bearing on your emotional problems, you see?"

"Oh. I'm sorry," Cherry said. She lay down on the couch again, and again Stuttgart placed his hand between her legs. He began stroking her there, as you would a pussy-cat, and although Cherry tried with all her might to keep herself in the proper clinical state of mind, she began to become sexually excited. Mentally, she berated herself for it. She told herself it was exactly the reason she needed to see a psychiatrist. She tried not to think of what the good doctor was doing. But her excitement only increased in intensity.

Suddenly she was startled by a glimpse over Stuttgart's shoulder at the toucan – as its beak lost its grip on the wire door and it banged shut again. Summoning all her willpower, she closed her eyes tightly and repeated over and over again to herself that she must not allow herself to be distracted by anything that might invalidate the doctor's tests.

"Relax, my dear," he encouraged. "Tell me what you feel must come out. Don't hold back. Let everything go." He spoke in the same soothing rhythms he was using to stroke her crotch.

She began to writhe and squirm a little. And because her breathing was heavy and irregular and her pulse was accelerated, when she began to express her innermost thoughts they came forth in a style that could be labeled *stream of conscious*. "I'm afraid...there's too much sex in my life...or too little...or too little of the right kind and too much of the wrong...I don't know what's the matter with me...I have a good job..."

"Too much sex? Or too little?" Dr. Stuttgart interjected.

"The pay is good...it's helping my boyfriend stay free to concentrate on his poetry...he's a genius and...Doctor...are you sure you're supposed to be doing this to me?"

"Absolutely."

"I mean, maybe...this kind of treatment...isn't right for my case."

She opened her eyes and again caught a glimpse of the wire door going shut.

"This is no *mere treatment,*" Stuttgart explained, taking umbrage. "I'm testing your reactions during stimulation, as a measure against your verbal and mental coordination. Please go on, Miss Jankowski...you were saying?"

"Sometimes I'm ashamed of myself. I shouldn't like sex so much. Or men. I shouldn't like men so much."

"Do you find this minor sexual stimulation exciting?" the doctor asked suddenly.

"Oh, yes, definitely...it's kind of...getting to me."

Stuttgart jumped up, removing his hand from her crotch, and she couldn't make up her mind whether she was relieved or disappointed, and also a fleeting thought passed through her mind that maybe she had done something unawares that would screw up the tests.

Unbeknownst to her, the good doctor had a throbbingly painful erection. He tried to hide it as he hobbled to the water cooler, crouching as low as he could, and he got another cup of water and tossed it down, splashing it on his coffee-stained shirt. Meantime, following his instructions, Cherry kept talking.

"I mean...there aren't any warm personal *relationships* any more. I try to be nice, but it always turns out that I'm taken advantage of."

Stuttgart returned to the couch, knelt down again, and cupped both her breasts in his hands and began massaging them.

Cherry knew by now that she wasn't supposed to mind this. "Like this guy next door," she said breathily. "He's a male chauvinist if there ever was one. He asks me to – oh, doctor, are you *sure* you're supposed to do..."

"Please continue. Continue."

"Well, I go up the ladder to help him with his draperies, and before you know it...he's got his you-know-what...inside...and then...and *now* for example...if this wasn't for scientific or medical purposes...well..."

She stopped talking because she could hardly talk anymore. She looked at Dr. Stuttgart, who was breathing heavily. He appeared to be ill or something.

"When is this test going to be over?" Cherry managed weakly.

Stuttgart leapt to his feet. "Give me your underthing!" he demanded.

"What!?"

"Your *underthing!*"

"What on earth! This *couldn't* be part of the test!"

"It most certainly is. Now, I *demand* you hand over your panties."

"Well...my god...I..."

"Now!"

Obediently, she removed her panties and handed them to the somewhat insane-looking doctor. She was skeptical of what he might be going to do with the panties. And she thought he was maybe a little eccentric. But her respect for his profession prevented her from analyzing the situation any further.

"Now, get on that exerciser and start pumping," he told her.

"But..."

"Do as I say!"

"What are we testing now?" she said quizzically.

"Verbal response in correlation to physical exertion. And keep talking!"

He moved briskly across the office and ducked into a small powder room. Leaving the door open a crack, he peeked out at Cherry as she got on the exerciser and began pedaling. She had her back to him. He had an excellent view of her bare bottom and the action of her luscious legs as they pumped up and down, up and down. He sniffed her panties, then covered his nose with them, breathing in deeply – and it intoxicated him. His eyes got glassy. He put the panties on over his head and looked at himself in the mirror. Then he began to masturbate, frantically, wildly, and did not hear when Cherry said, in a continuation of her self-analytical monologue, "I *love* Herman...I mean...he has such a beautiful mind. But I'm sort of a physical person...and...I guess he's right...I'm full of wild, unspeakable lusts..."

And the good doctor did not hear any more of what Cherry had to say, because, sad to say, he was soon lost in the throes of his climax – which came to him with a sudden shuddering convulsion – and caused him to inadvertently slam the bathroom door shut on his fingers. Cherry couldn't help being startled by his scream, and she covered her face with her hands, in the expectation that the toucan had gotten loose and would fly at her – but nothing of that sort actually happened, and she soon realized that it was Stuttgart who had done the screaming. She listened for a while without talking or pumping the exerciser, then she called out tentatively, "Are you all right, Dr. Stuttgart?"

But there was no answer. Just the sound of water running. And then a commode flushing. And then, when Dr. Stuttgart came out, two of his fingers were bandaged. But he seemed serious and well-composed. And he handed Cherry her panties.

"You may go now," he said perfunctorily.

"I feel that I'm worthless," Cherry confessed. "I don't deserve to be loved. My boyfriend is too good for me."

"Quit your job," Stuttgart advised.

"You think so?" Cherry said, amazed. She could not see what connection her job at Joyful could possibly have with her mental and emotional problems.

"Yes," Stuttgart said. "That is all for today. You may pay me fifty dollars."

Cherry went over to the couch and got her purse and paid him the money. He stuffed the wrinkled bills into his pants pocket. And she climbed into her panties while he watched with an aloof attitude (because he had no interest in her now that he had been self-gratified). He went to the water cooler.

And Cherry let herself out into the reception area, and Miss Peabody smiled at her constantly as she left the office and made her way toward the elevators.

Cherry was so confused that she kept turning everything over and over in her mind. Her vagina was wet and unsatisfied. Still, she felt an inner glow of satisfaction that she had taken the major step of going to see a psychiatrist, and she felt reasonably sure that it was the first step on the road to mental health and peace of mind.

As she got on one of the twin elevators and pressed a button for the lobby, a coincidence happened: her elevator door went shut and she began descending, just as Marcello Fettucini stepped off the other elevator – and they narrowly missed seeing each other. They were "ships in the night," so to speak, both in the midst of a similar mission.

Marcello, too, had an appointment with Dr. Julius Stuttgart. Nervously glancing all around, as if he might bump into someone who would laugh at him for going to a psychiatrist, he walked down the hall and, summoning his courage, opened the door to Stuttgart's office.

CHAPTER 24

FETTUCINI, MARCELLO
AGE: 27
SEX: MALE
WOULD NOT DISCUSS HIS PROBLEM
OVER THE PHONE

Miss Cornelia Peabody typed out Marcello's preliminary information on a three-by-five card, and smiled at him as she showed him the way to Dr. Stuttgart's office. Marcello tried to thank her politely, but his tongue stuck to the roof of his mouth and only a squeak came out, which he hoped she did not hear.

Luckily there was a water cooler. Dr. Stuttgart walked in while Marcello was in the middle of gargling, and said, "Yes, yes, Marcello! Sit down, won't you please?"

Marcello sat down on the couch, and Dr. Stuttgart sat down beside him. "Tell me your problem," the psychiatrist encouraged. "Don't be afraid...let everything come out. After all, I can't help you unless I know everything that's on your mind."

"Scusa," Marcello said, reverting to partial use of his native Italian, as he always did when he was exceptionally agitated. He cleared his throat, and as he did this his eyes fell on the toucan in its smelly cage – and the bird had the cage door partially opened, and it looked to Marcello as though the darned thing was about to escape.

"That-a parrot, it no canna get out. No?"

"No," Stuttgart said. And he went to the cage, slammed the wire door shut on the bird's claws, and used his sharp pencil to poke the bird toward the rear of the cage. All this was accompanied by a flurry of irate squawking from the toucan, which caused Dr. Stuttgart to smile.

Marcello was somewhat puzzled by the whole thing. But he figured that the doctor probably needed the parrot for his experiments. And besides, Marcello had no particular sympathy for the bird anyhow. To tell you otherwise would be a lie; and I'm not going to resort to such a lie just to falsely encourage your empathy for one of my lead characters.

Stuttgart again took his place on the couch. He said, "Go on, Marcello. You were saying?"

"Nothing."

"Well, go on...let's get on with it."

Marcello sucked in his breath deeply and let out a long, lingering sigh. "My problem is-a *terrible*," he said finally. "It is-a no laughing matter."

"No one is going to laugh at you," Stuttgart promised, with a smile. "Why, some of the cases I've heard would shock the daylights out of you. In my years of practice I've been privy to just about everything known to man – or woman. For instance a female client of mine used to masturbate with an electric alarm clock – an old one that whirred and vibrated. And there was a young lady in here just before you who was so confused you just wouldn't believe it. So feel free to tell me your problem. That's what you're paying me for. And I can't help you unless you speak up."

Once again Marcello sucked in his breath and let it out with a deep sigh. "Women donna excite me anymore," he said, and the silence that followed his statement crashed around his ears as if he had just made the most awesome pronouncement in the history of the earth.

But Dr. Stuttgart merely smiled reassuringly. And he put his hand on Marcello's right leg, in a friendly way. And Marcello noticed the bandages on Dr. Stuttgart's fingers, as the doctor began to rub his hand on the inner part of Marcello's thigh.

"Marcello, you are from a foreign country," the doctor began. "And it is therefore natural, you see, for you to worry about some things that no longer bother our modern, educated people here in America. Latent homosexual tendencies are nothing for you to be ashamed of. Incest, homosexuality, lesbianism, pederasty, are all perfectly acceptable nowadays. You shouldn't try to stifle your natural urges...let them come out...give them free expression...it is clear to me that you are a bisexual person..."

At that point the doctor's bandaged fingers were about to reach Marcello's crotch – and Miss Cornelia Peabody was interrupted in the midst of her typing by the most horrendous racket and screams of anguish she had ever heard in this sedate office. *Human* SCREAMS! All coming from behind Dr. Stuttgart's closed office door.

And then Marcello Fettucini stormed right by Miss Peabody in a huff, and before she could even decide whether or not to smile at him, he stomped out of the office, slamming the door behind him. "That brute!" Miss Peabody thought. "That brute has done something unthinkable!"

She crept along the wall and peered cautiously into Dr. Stuttgart's office, and what she saw brought a scream to her throat that choked itself off and would have become a laugh or a giggle if she had not controlled herself by biting her upper lip until it nearly started bleeding. Don't get me wrong, she felt sorry for Dr. Stuttgart, but at the same time it was amusing to see him crawling on the floor, thrashing around like a blind man, while trying to remove the office wastebasket from his head – but it was on too tight and his head had apparently been jammed into it.

"Oh, my!" Miss Peabody managed finally. "Oh, my, Dr. Stuttgart...are you all right?"

She couldn't tell if he was all right or not, because all she could hear from inside the wastebasket was muffled mumbling which sounded like curse words. "Do you want me to call the police?" she asked the good doctor, because it was all she could think of.

"Elf me wid did wafebasked," the muffled voice said.

"What?"

"WAFEBASKED!!"

Dutifully, and immeasurably glad, for the sake of her job, that Dr. Stuttgart couldn't see the smile on her face, Miss Peabody took a firm hold on the rim of the wastebasket and tried to be of some help. But it wouldn't budge. And she had to bite her tongue again when she saw the bandages on Dr. Stuttgart's fingers.

CHAPTER 25

Meanwhile, Cherry Jankowski was being raped. Or, rather, an attempt was being made in that direction, but the would-be rapist, luckily, was an incredible bungler. It happened this way:

On her way home from Stuttgart's office, Cherry tried to save time by cutting through an alley, and a man leaped out at her brandishing a shotgun and wearing a Halloween mask that looked like Moe of the Three Stooges. "Uh...this is a stickup," the man said. "Uh...no...this is a rape. Take your panties off and lift up your skirt."

Cherry swooned and passed out, which was a break for the rapist, who had been wondering how he was going to keep the shotgun on her and still conduct a sexual encounter, and he was sorry he had not brought a knife with him. But now that didn't matter. Gratefully, he knelt over the unconscious girl and hiked her skirt up and removed her panties, glowing with the realization of his good fortune when he realized how gorgeous she was. Even so, her being out cold was going to spoil things a little because he would have to do all the work himself. He didn't mind that so much, but he sort of missed the pleasure of putting a gun or knife to his victims' heads and giving them the order to "fuck their brains out," which was his usual style.

It exasperated him when his zipper stuck. He tugged at it. Struggled with it. Swore at it. And was just about to tear his trousers open, when a stray dog wandered into the alley and came over and sniffed at the would-be rapist's crotch.

Indignantly, he said, "Go away, you stupid mutt!"

97

The dog pushed its nose up against the rapist's testicles and sniffed again.

"Get away! Get away!"

It is a nasty habit that some dogs have, along with humping people's legs, but this time it benefitted Cherry.

A window went up.

A lady started screaming.

Cherry regained consciousness, moaning softly, as if awakened from a nightmare.

And the would-be rapist grabbed up his shotgun and zipped up his zipper and fled out of the alley. Well, he fled as fast as he could flee, although he was limping somewhat due to the ache in his testicles caused by too much unrewarded sexual stimulation.

CHAPTER 26

"Fantasy! Pure fantasy!" Dr. Stuttgart said. "My dear, I'm afraid you've gone from bad to worse."

He had his thumb inside Cherry's vagina.

"But...but it was so *real,*" she muttered, half-pleadingly.

Dr. Stuttgart's hand went to his forehead, where he gingerly probed the bandage that had been put there by Miss Peabody after the encounter with that brute of a patient, Marcello Fettucini. Stuttgart had been forced to get the janitor up here to remove the wastebasket from his head, and he was still smarting from the embarrassment.

"Dreams can capture the body and soul," he told Cherry, bored by his own words because he had spoken them so many times to so many clients. "You are a victim of your own wild, lustful imagination. A common phenomenon. I had a fine upstanding lady once, a society lady, who used to dream of screwing fire hydrants. And you wouldn't believe the animal I had in here just a short while ago. When I refused to let him seduce me, he bashed me over the head with my own wastebasket."

Cherry's eyes widened, and she said musingly, "Then it can actually happen? The mind playing tricks on a person?"

"Unquestionably."

"But it seemed so *real*. He was trying to rape me, and he had a dog with him."

"Oh, yes, quite a fantasy," said Stuttgart. "But I'm not going to charge you the full amount, since this is your second visit here today. You may pay me forty-five dollars, a five-dollar rebate."

He picked up Cherry's panties and tucked them in his vest pocket, then told her, "I found no evidence of rape, no penetration when I probed with my thumb. But I'll keep your panties and send them to the FBI Laboratory in Washington. Maybe they can find something. I'll let you know the results of their tests."

"Thank you so much, Doctor," Cherry said, truly grateful, and she paid him and left the office and the ever-smiling Miss Peabody, as Dr. Stuttgart opened his file cabinet and deposited her panties inside and locked them up for future reference.

CHAPTER 27

On a Thursday, Stag the janitor was overjoyed to find that the morning mail contained a package for him in a plain brown wrapper. Oh, jolly good! He just knew it was his replacement artificial vagina. He unwrapped it while the milk he needed to pour into it was warming in a saucepan on the electric stove. The milk was to be poured inside the artificial apparatus, according to instructions, so that the rubber would warm up and soften to feel like real human flesh. Stag didn't like milk, because he had lactose intolerance, and he hated to think how many spoiled cartons of it he had had to flush down the sink during the past few weeks as he waited daily, and anxiously, for his artificial vagina to arrive. Also, every time he walked into a supermarket to buy a carton of milk, his face turned red and he stammered excessively, as if he were buying a pack of prophylactics.

Now his replacement artificial vagina was actually here, and he couldn't wait to try it out! He felt like a man with a mail-order bride.

There was a note in the bottom of the package, thanking him for his patience and kindness in not cancelling his order and hoping that his brand-new Joyful Artificial Vagina would provide him with many delightful evenings of erotic entertainment. While he waited for the milk to heat up, Stag squeezed the rubber bulb a few times, which made the disembodied vagina flex and un-flex, rhythmically, or in whatever tempo one chose to squeeze the rubber bulb. It lacked the essential quality of a real woman, in that one cannot so easily manipulate her reactions, but Stag wasn't one to nitpick. Looking at his new toy and reading the instructions gave him a tremendous erection.

He stripped naked and, looking at himself in his bedroom mirror, he admired the huge pulsating mass of his nine-inch penis and the large hairy testicles hanging down underneath. Then he rummaged through his dresser drawer for his deck of Joyful playing cards and removed the ones showing fellatio and cunnilingus, which were on the top of the deck. By then, he couldn't wait any longer. He uncapped his artificial vagina and filled it with lukewarm milk.

"Damn that Cherry Jankowski," he said to himself silently. He liked to talk to himself inside his mind because that way he never stuttered.

"Damn that Cherry Jankowski," he said again. "Who n-n-needs h-h-h-her."

Inadvertently he had spoken that last sentence out loud as he dove into bed and pulled the covers up over himself and his Joyful Artificial Vagina.

CHAPTER 28

Cherry summoned all her courage and pounded with both her fists on the door to Biggs' apartment. The door opened and Biggs poked his head out and Cherry began shouting at him.

"The thing you did the other day was *disgusting*! I tried to be nice, and you acted like a wild beast! I *demand* an apology!"

"Why don't you come inside and we'll talk about it," Biggs said, politely.

"Well, if you think you can talk about it in a *civilized* manner..."

"Surely," Biggs said, as he opened the door wider and ushered Cherry inside. "I don't know what got into me the other day. I guess I've been down in the dumps lately, I'm going through such a rough spot in my life."

Cherry began to feel sorry for him.

Noting this, he went on. "Yesterday, this war wound in my arm began acting up again. The doctor found more shrapnel."

He did indeed have a bandage on his arm, and it made Cherry feel even more sorry for him. She remembered an article she had skimmed over in *Time* magazine which dwelled on some of the problems common to returning veterans. Some of them came back from the war with sex hang-ups and hang-ups unrelated to sex, and the article had stressed the need for patience to be exercised by the people welcoming them home so they would have time and tender loving care enough to slowly recover.

Biggs was just sick, Cherry thought, and probably needed a little human kindness.

"Would you mind closing the door for me?" he asked as they paused in the center of his living room.

She did so, and Biggs' good hand shot up to his eye and he screamed out, "Ow! Damn it!"

"What's the matter?!" Cherry shrieked.

"My contact lens. It popped out onto the floor. You'll have to help me look for it."

Cherry eyed him skeptically as he stood there holding his eye. "Are you sure I can trust you, Vernon?"

"I can't even see, for Chrissake!"

Cherry got down on her hands and knees and began crawling around looking for the lost contact lens. And Biggs got down on the floor with her. Crawling behind her, he could not help but notice how enticingly her skirt was hiked up, and how underneath it she was not wearing any panties, and how, as she moved, her buttocks undulated ever so invitingly and exposed the point of entry between her legs.

"I can't feel anything," Cherry said. "The carpet is too thick. I don't think we'll ever find it. *Oh!"*

She called out sharply just then, for Biggs had grabbed her around her waist and jammed his penis in her from behind. It happened so very quickly that Cherry was taken totally by surprise – and victimized. Biggs began to saw away inside her. She squirmed and struggled – and the wide-eyed look on her face began to melt away...into the dreamy yet guilty expression that is to be found on persons who are receiving sexual attentions which they have not solicited but which are turning out to be pleasurable nonetheless.

(NOTE: Dear Reader, I am not in any way condoning the despicable behavior of Vernon Biggs. And I know full well that women should not be made the culprit or the enticer when they are victimized by rapists or otherwise brutish men. Cherry is a very selective case, and is not meant to represent womankind in general. She is her own worst enemy, and psychologically inept to the point where she gets herself in sticky situations. I must admit that she is oversexed and uninhibited and subconsciously desirous of the sexual attentions that she pretends not to want. The vast majority of women are not that way, and all men need to understand this. If you read on, you will find out how in the end dear Cherry resolves her personal problems satisfactorily.)

Cherry was outraged by Biggs' behavior, truly. Yet she was only human, and a penis moving inside a vagina will produce pleasurable sensations in time, as a matter of immutable biological law. This does not in any way absolve Biggs or make him any less the villain. No, I'm not trying to say that. But I am trying to render an account of what happened and how the people felt, as completely and fairly as possible.

It is to Cherry's credit that she continued to protest almost to the bitter end, albeit weakly, because of the pleasurable sexual stimulation that was being forced on her. "Oh, you... Vernon Biggs... you are the most... most... despicable person..." And as Biggs continued to saw away inside her, she yielded finally to the tensions of her mounting orgasm, but not before promising herself that she would give him a good piece of her mind when it was all over.

As for Biggs, he was wallowing in low-down, illicit satisfaction. His five-inch penis was swollen to the maximum, as it dived and plunged inside Cherry's honey-pot – and his ecstatic grunts and moans were overheard by Stag the janitor, who had been using a push-broom out on the landing but stopped sweeping immediately and put his ear to the door to listen.

"Unh! Unh! *Unh!* Egad!" Stag heard through the closed apartment door, as Biggs ejaculated and threw himself down across Cherry's back as wave after wave of pleasure shot through him and his penis shrunk and flopped out of her.

Stag listened intently but heard no more. But all that he *had* heard made him quite randy, and so, leaving his push-broom leaning against the wall, he ran down to his room and got into bed with his Joyful Artificial Vagina.

CHAPTER 29

"Fettucini has failed again! Bring in a replacement!"

The Chief Engineer's angry voice reverberated inside the confines of Test Lab B, causing Marcello to smart with embarrassment. His penis hung in limp testimony to his failure, as he began pulling on his robe.

The engineers and aides stared at him with the open contempt that technicians always feel for something that won't operate efficiently.

Her feelings hurt, the Female Tester sat up on the bed and pouted. "Aren't I good enough for him? Is he stuck-up or something?"

"He's not sticking up at all," the Chief Engineer said, and the aides snickered. To the Female Tester, he spoke consolingly. "Relax. Lie down and take it easy, till we call up a replacement. This is Marcello's nineteenth erection failure. So it's not just you. *Nobody* can get it up for him."

"You've done all that's humanly possible," an assistant engineer added. "The blame rests squarely on Marcello's shoulders."

"Well, he's got a lot of nerve!" the Female Tester said. "Who does he think he is, anyway!"

"Lie back, don't let it bother you," the Chief Engineer cajoled. "We'll have a replacement up here in a few minutes. If you don't calm yourself, it will have an adverse effect on your performance."

Theophilus Suck came striding in, accompanied by the replacement Male Tester, a young man nude except for a white towel around his loins. "What's going on here?" Suck demanded. "Another erection failure?"

"Fettucini's got a tired weenie," the replacement Male Tester snickered, and he whipped off his towel to reveal his own huge, throbbing erection. He waved it mockingly at Marcello.

Marcello glowered and made a clenched fist, but the replacement Male Tester merely laughed and took his place on the testing bed, between the legs of the Female Tester.

"I didda my best...I...I," Marcello stammered, when Suck got in his face.

"Apparently your best is not good enough," Suck said, contemptuously. "I want you to take the rest of the day off, without pay. Maybe if we dock you enough times you'll wise up. And get it up. Tomorrow morning you report to my office, first thing."

Marcello hung his head and shuffled lamely out of the room, as Suck turned to have a confidential word with his engineers. "Is there any reason you can see why a normal person wouldn't be able to achieve an erection?" Suck asked.

The Chief Engineer said, "He was given every chance, boss. You name it, he had it done. Fellatio, anilingus, the works. I think he needs a psychiatrist."

"Sad, so sad," said Suck.

"I don't know the answer," the Chief Engineer said. "I wish I could tell you otherwise. When does his contract expire? Are we married to him?"

"There's a termination clause," Suck said. "If he doesn't perform, we have the right to fire him. The Product Testers Union can't do a thing for him. I was hoping it wouldn't come to that, but it appears we may not have any choice. He's costing us too much in down time, and I don't need to tell you how it affects you all when it comes to profit sharing."

"I still think he needs a psychiatrist," one of the aides said. "I gave him an excellent recommendation – Dr. Julius Stuttgart – he worked wonders with my own daughter when she got married and had a bout with frigidity."

"Somebody needs to help him straighten out his mental block," agreed the Chief Engineer. "I believe his penis is normal. His problem is all in his head."

They all nodded their heads in solemn agreement, and Suck turned on his heels and walked out of the lab. He was thinking that his cat-and-mouse game with Marcello had become a costly diversion and maybe this time he should end it for sure. But his thoughts were interrupted by his receptionist, who met him in the hall and handed him a package that had arrived by parcel post. Suck thanked her for it, and noticed that it was ticking.

He gave it a shake. It kept ticking.

There was a return address. The package had been sent by someone named Angelo Fettucini. Suck understood. A wry smile played across his lips. Probably a box of cookies from Marcello's family, designed to curry favor for Marcello. If the dumb dagos thought a box of cookies --

Then why was it ticking?

If the box exploded, even the name and the return address might be obliterated and would not remain as evidence.

Theophilus Suck broke out in a cold sweat. Handling the package as gingerly as he could, he walked briskly to the receptionist's desk and asked her to please open it for him. She took it, and he hot-footed it down the hall, headed for the far side of the building.

The receptionist put her cup of coffee aside, picked up the package and gave it a good shake, as she always did before opening a present, trying to guess what was inside.

It began ringing.

She opened it and found an inexpensive alarm clock with the price-tag still on it. It stopped ringing when the alarm wound down, and she took it to Suck's office and left it on his desk. She threw away the box it had come in, and did not see the folded note in the bottom under some wrapping paper, where it had fallen when the box had been shaken. The note was composed of letters cut from old newspapers and this was its message:

YOU DON'T KNOW ME BUT I KNOW YOU.
I GOT MY EYE ON YOU.
YOU WAS LUCKY ENOUGH TO ESCAPE
THE KNIFE BUT MAYBE NEXT TIME
YOU AIN'T GONNA BE SO LUCKY.
DIS CHOULD BE FOOD FOR THOUGHT.
LAY OFF OF MARCELLO OR NEXT TIME
I DON'T SEND JUST A CLOCK.
GET ME?

Suck jumped when he entered his office and saw the clock on his desk, but it was no longer ticking and did not explode. With relief, since circumstances kept him from seeing the note, he thought it was merely a cheap clock and nothing more. A wry smile came to his lips. Leave it to the dumb wops. If they thought he was going to be lenient with Marcello just because they gave him a cheap clock, they had another think coming. A box of cookies would've been nicer, but still would not have bought any favors.

Suck snickered. He was a stern and ruthless man when it came to running Joyful Novelties, Inc. And he knew it had to be that way. The profit motive demanded it. Any sort of favoritism had to be eliminated.

Just to be on the safe side where the scary little clock was concerned, Suck made a present of it to his receptionist who, if anything bad were to happen to her, she wasn't as highly paid or as valuable as his product testers and engineers. He figured that giving her the present was good for employer-employee relations. And, for her own part, she was diplomatic enough to thank him for it, then she took it home after work and threw it away.

CHAPTER 30

Cherry had one good, true confidante at Joyful: Thelma Bartholomew. Thelma had spent her younger years as a product tester, but she was past sixty now and worked most of the time in the shipping department, which was an unexciting job, but a necessary one, and one which had given her leisure in her declining years to look back over her career philosophically and with a view toward helping young girls like Cherry not to make some of the same mistakes that she herself had made in her youth, when she had been, like Cherry, terribly impressionable and with a body that men lusted after.

(I must digress here and reveal to you, in the interest of candidness, that Thelma was the Joyful employee who had sent Mr. Stag the wrong size artificial vagina, but she wasn't the only person working in the shipping department at that time, and so no one, including her, was blamed for the error, which would have embarrassed her if she had been wise to her own mistake.)

Cherry did not always have the insight to recognize when she needed some good, solid advice, and so she did not ask Thelma for it very often, and Thelma had the sense not to offer it when she was not asked, because she realized that nothing builds resentment in people better than good advice when it comes unsolicited. One particular afternoon, though, while Cherry had a few moments off between sessions of product testing, and Thelma was occupied but not totally absorbed in the task of painting the tips of dildos red and then packing them as they dried, to get them ready for shipment, Cherry came in and sat down, and she and Thelma had a good heart-to-heart talk. And it all began after Cherry, with a great deal of hesitation and considerable fumbling around and false-starting, confessed that she had been to a famous psychiatrist, and he had advised her to quit her job.

Thelma had long hoped that Cherry would resign her position at Joyful, as she believed it would be in Cherry's best interest and would do her a world of good – but she had never mentioned this to Cherry because she knew it was the kind of realization that could never be *effectively told* to anyone, but that person had to realize it independently, out of his or her own personal experience. Now that the idea had been planted in Cherry's mind, however, by a professional person whom she respected, Thelma hastened to reinforce it and render it incontrovertible.

"I don't know why any of us put up with this shit," Thelma began. "I've had lots of misery down through the years. Doctor bills. Female trouble. Even now, when I don't test anything anymore."

Cherry listened attentively while Thelma gestured angrily at the row of dildos with their tips painted red which were drying on the table in front of her. The shade of red was not very life-like, Cherry thought.

"You go home after handling two thousand of these things," Thelma said, "and I guarantee you, you don't feel like getting laid. You can't stand looking at one more pecker, real or imagined."

"But," Cherry said, "I would've thought --"

"I know, dear, you think I'm too old. You've got a lot to learn. Change of life turns you *on* – not off. You don't have to worry about getting knocked up anymore. You don't have to tinker around with pills or contraptions. After age sixty is when you can start having *carefree* sex!"

"Herman says I should read more," Cherry interjected. "I'm dumb. He's too good for me."

"Does *he* tell you that?"

"He doesn't have to. He's brilliant. You should hear his poetry."

"How is he in the sack?" Thelma asked.

"Well..."

"Sometimes fancy words help put you in the mood, but you gotta have *action* when it gets down to the nitty-gritty," Thelma said.

"Herman's going to be *wonderful*," Cherry sighed, with an effort at convincing Thelma. "But we've agreed I should save myself for him till after we're married."

Thelma's mouth dropped open and she was so taken aback that she smeared red paint on her index finger. "You gotta be kiddin'," she said with a flush of amazement. "Any guy that don't wanna screw a gal like you is messed up in the head or somethin'."

"Herman's *sensitive*, he's a *poet*," Cherry said. She was beginning to think maybe Thelma shouldn't be her friend anymore, because she was obviously too coarse and ignorant to understand deep and noble feelings.

"The most sensitive thing on a real man is between his legs," Thelma said. "Time for lunch, honey."

Cherry watched while Thelma used turpentine to clean red paint from her fingers.

Suddenly the door banged open and Mr. Suck entered, glancing around and looking terribly upset. "We can't find Marcello!" he said, exasperated. "He was scheduled to do a test with you this afternoon, and he seems to be nowhere in the building. He was supposed to report for a preliminary checkup."

"Did you look in the john?" Thelma asked. "Sometimes he mopes in there. When he comes out in the open some of the jerks around here make fun of him."

"We've looked everywhere," Suck said with a look of desperation. "His locker is empty. We had to cut it open with a blowtorch. Did he say anything to you about quitting?"

"No," Cherry said.

"Nothing," said Thelma.

Suddenly a terrible thought flashed through Cherry's mind. She trembled, remembering Marcello's wild talk about committing suicide.

"Your test for today has been cancelled," Suck told her. "This sort of thing can't go on – we're trying to operate a *business*."

"I know. I'm sorry," Cherry said.

"It's not your fault, dear," Thelma comforted.

Suck lost his temper. "The stupid goddamn dago! This time I'm gonna fire him for sure!" He pivoted and went out the door, slamming it behind him.

"Well, ain't you the lucky stiff?" Thelma said, winking at Cherry. "Now you've got the rest of the day off. You can go home and unwind."

"No," Cherry said. "I can't go home. Herman likes to be alone when he's writing."

"He sounds like a real creep," Thelma said.

"Don't talk about him that way!" Cherry said. "He's working on a book of poetry! Beautiful poetry! Tremendously inspiring!"

"Remember what I told you, honey. If he won't put his thing in you, it means he doesn't really love you."

Cherry lapsed into contemplative silence as Thelma put the turpentine away and the two of them walked to the lunch room together.

CHAPTER 31

In the afternoon mail, Herman received crushing news from his agent:

Dear Mr. Longfellow:

I am returning your manuscript forthwith. I have faithfully tried to decipher it and find in it some trace of literary merit, but I have failed. I am a busy man, and I find I can no longer devote myself to your interests. Therefore, I urge you to find someone who might serve you better.

Sincerely,
Dwight Armbruster Sperry
Literary Agent

Severely traumatized, Herman started the gas logs burning in the fireplace and fed Dwight Armbruster Sperry's derisive note into the flames. He did this with a numb and glazed look in his eyes.

Then he got into drag, because "dressing up" was his secret panacea for any deep emotional crisis. Totally distracted and mostly unaware of what he was doing, he found himself leaving the apartment in his female getup – the first time he had "come out" publicly. He meandered to the corner drugstore and purchased a large bottle of sleeping pills. The pharmacist recognized Herman and made small talk about how much fun it was to go to a costume party not just on Halloween but on any day of the year. But Herman's mind was in such a tizzy that he paid for the sleeping pills with a twenty-dollar bill and absent-mindedly allowed himself to be short-changed by five dollars. And out on the street he got hit up by a Salvation Army lady with a tambourine, who pinned a plastic flower over his artificial breast after he fumbled in his purse and gave her fifty cents.

Back at the door to Cherry's apartment, Herman got stared at by Stag the janitor, who happened to be on the landing with a push-broom, and after he entered, he sat on the bed and contemplated swallowing the pills. Committing suicide in this manner had an allure for him because it was the method traditionally favored by glamorous movie queens. His psyche was both tortured and tantalized by a vision of himself sprawled on the bed in his gown and wig, blessed with the nobility and grace of death, his literary genius recognized too late by the busy and cruel world which had been so unwilling to pay him homage while he was still alive. The scenario was romantic and touching.

The unromantic thing about it was the vomiting. Herman had read that death by an overdose of sleeping pills was invariably preceded by massive vomiting, and he found it impossible to be enamored of that aspect of it. The image of being found dead and caked with vomit did not enthrall him. Also, upon sitting behind his typewriter to compose a suicide note, he found that his mind was too jangled to find words noble and true enough to express his dying sentiments. He did not wish to exit the world on the wings of doggerel.

The upshot was that he flushed the sleeping pills down the toilet, after taking two of them so he could get to sleep.

He resolved before shutting his eyes not to mention the letter from Dwight Armbruster Sperry to Cherry Jankowski. He had doubts about her ability to understand that this latest rejection was not a reflection upon his talent but a barometer of the tastelessness and iniquity of the world at large. And if he did not kill himself until some future date, in the meantime he would need Cherry's support so he could go on writing.

Thus tormented, Herman came under the influence of the two sleeping pills, a modest dose, and dozed off.

CHAPTER 32

Meanwhile Marcello Fettucini was composing a suicide note of his own, by dictating it into a Korean tape recorder that he had bought for thirty dollars in a pawn shop around the corner from Joyful Novelties, Inc. All his efforts to become virile again had dismally failed, and he had resigned himself to the fact that his life might as well be over.

Now, with resignation, had come a curious objectivity and detachment that was almost exhilarating – and Marcello was sitting in bed naked, smoking a De Nobili cigar, as he gazed all about him at shreds and tatters of pornographic pictures which had failed to stimulate his penis to erect itself and which he had torn into bits and pieces before getting into bed and making the final, irrevocable decision to commit suicide.

With a sweeping histrionic gesture that he endeavored to make as fateful and dramatic as the final act of Brutus in falling on his sword, Marcello pressed the "record" button on the tape recorder, but the machine had never worked for the person who had pawned it, and was not working now – in other words it was not really recording anything, so unfortunately the text of his suicide oration is lost to posterity. The salient aspects of it were that he wanted to will his body to science for study, so that his terrible condition might not befall other young men in the prime of life, and he wished to have the ashes of his cremated body returned to Italy and scattered over the Roman ruins.

He put all he had into his speech, then re-wound the tape and attempted to play it back, only to find that nothing had been recorded. He shook the machine, pounded on it, cursed it in Italian, all to no avail. The tape kept turning around with no sound coming out of it but the squeak of the plastic reels.

With a helpless shrug, Marcello got out of bed, took a shave and shower and put on his best suit and tie, and went out to do himself in.

***

Around midnight, Theophilus Suck was awakened by the ringing of his telephone. He let it ring for a long time, waiting for his wife Evangeline to answer it, but when he reached over to poke her in the ribs he found that she was not in bed. "Oh, for chrissake, she's out carousing and has had an accident!" was his first thought, and a mixture of annoyance and relief at the thought of Evangeline's death swept over him as he reached for the telephone.

It turned out to be his Chief Engineer on the night shift, who said, "There's been accident, boss."

"Yes?"

"One of the product testers. We were testing the XX20 Ultravibrator on her and it was going really great for a while – she must've had fifty orgasms in the space of five minutes. But she never came out of it, boss – *heart* failure."

"So why are you calling me at this hour?" Suck said.

"Uh...but...I thought you'd want to know about it."

"Did you phone the doctor?"

"No..."

"Well, *call him!*"

"But...she's dead. What good could a doctor do? You should see the pleasant smile on her face, though, boss. The XX20 is gonna be a big hit, if we can get the bugs ironed out."

"I know, I know. But call the doctor. He's got to fill out the death certificate. Otherwise, we might get sued. Now get on the stick and let me get some sleep."

"Right, boss," the Chief Engineer said, but Theophilus did not hear because he had already hung up.

Sleep.

Theophilus was certain he'd probably not be able to get back to sleep. Too many business problems.

Where the hell was Evangeline?

He lit up a cigarette and smoked while he entertained himself with mind pictures of her fat body smashed up in her Cadillac, the car accordionated against a concrete wall, her cracked peroxided head protruding through the shattered windshield. He could not restrain the feeling that in many ways his life would be more comfortable with her gone. The pressure would be off, sexually. She still wanted it, and he was no longer interested. Maybe it was because he had been surrounded with an excess of it for his entire career.

Anyway, he might as well look for her and make sure she was safely in the house.

Going down the hall, he heard screams and moans from his mentally challenged son's bedroom, so he peeked in.

He shook his head in an amused way when he saw his wife going wildly up and down in her naked passion, as Abraham grunted and heaved beneath her.

CHAPTER 33

Marcello Fettucini stood alone in the middle of a high suspension bridge, looking down at the river coursing far below. In the distance he could see the neon lights of the city, and could hear a few strains of a jukebox tune or an occasional cry of pain or laughter. But he felt no connection with the rest of humanity now. He was alone. Even the cars and trucks that barreled across the bridge, splashing his trousers with wet mud, seemed to serve as a reminder of his total and final alienation from the world.

Yes, Marcello had all these kinds of thoughts as he stood on the bridge looking down into oblivion. The realization that he would soon be dead filled him with sadness, as if he would still be around to mourn himself after he was gone. He could picture his long brown hair streaming in the wind on the way down, like an angel he had once seen in a painting by Boticelli.

He tantalized himself with visions of his swan dive into eternity, unaware that a certain amount of disillusionment would be inevitable if he opened his eyes on the way down and saw the garbage and oily scum floating on the polluted river.

But he could not see the garbage and oily scum from high on the bridge, and his brain was entranced by transcendental and ennobling thoughts as he took several steps back from the railing and a monstrous diesel truck splashed him with muddy water from a pothole. He slapped his right bicep with the palm of his left hand and yelled "Bahfongool!" after the truck, and then carefully removed his shoes and socks and his suit and tie and shirt and trousers, and folded them neatly in a pile.

Totally nude, he knelt at the rail, blessed himself with the Sign of the Cross, and began to say a Hail Mary. But he could not remember all the words, and the gritty concrete was beginning to hurt his knees, and he decided to fudge it and go on to the next verse – but just then a big, burly policeman stepped up behind him and laid a heavy hand on his shoulder.

"Nice evening for a swim, eh, Bub," the cop said.

"Uh...I was-a...uh...*pardone*...uh...*scusa...I...*" Marcello replied.

"That water down there is cold as a witch's tit," the cop warned. "And it's polluted with garbage. Maybe we oughta give you a night in the jug to think it over."

"But...I no canna go to jail," Marcello said. "Tomorrow I must-a look-a for a new job."

"You ain't gonna find no new job at the bottom of that river," the cop said. "Get your clothes on, bub, before I change my mind and book you for indecent exposure."

CHAPTER 34

Herman Longfellow was snoring loudly, drugged by pills and fatigued emotionally by the output of energy it had taken to withstand his literary disappointments, so he did not hear a thing when Cherry came into the bedroom after work and stood over him, eyeing him lovingly and longing for him sexually because she had been primed earlier to have sex at Joyful, and then her test had been cancelled because Marcello was a no-show.

She took all her clothes off and was nude and beautiful. Her nipples were erect with the thought of making love to her boyfriend. She trembled at the idea of his virile body under the quilt, and her lusts reached a fever pitch when she allowed her mind to dwell upon fantasies of his huge hairy testicles and his penis the size of a fire hydrant. She was so consumed with lust at this moment that logic and restraint deserted her in favor of pornographic exaggeration. She knew that Herman's penis could not be as big as a fire hydrant, yet thinking about it that way fired her up and turned her into a wanton animal. She licked her lips. Then she cupped her right breast in her left hand, while her right hand moved to the mound between her legs and stroked it a few times and inserted her finger. A lewd smile played across her moistened lips as a deliciously mischievous idea struck her and almost made her giggle in spite of the highly pleasurable sensations that her fingers were bringing to her stiffening little clitoris. The idea was this: she was going to perform fellatio on Herman while he was asleep.

Kneeling naked at the edge of the bed, she began pulling carefully on the quilt to reveal Herman's nakedness.

But he wasn't naked.

He was dressed up like a woman!

Cherry shrieked as, in a state of wide-eyed shock she let the edge of the quilt drop out of her hand.

Herman did not awaken. He was still snoring loudly. Impulsively she shook him by his shoulders. "Herman!" she cried. "Wake up, Herman!"

"Huh? What?" he said in his drowsiness. He had been having a nice dream that one of his poems had been purchased by the Library of Congress, with the intention of having it set to music as the new National Anthem.

He opened his eyes but closed them immediately when he realized that his secret was out: his penchant for dressing up, his leaning toward being a member of the opposite sex. He tried to think of a plausible excuse for his feminine getup, but failed. He closed his eyes tighter when he saw the rosy pink nipples of Cherry's breasts staring him in the face.

She said, "I'm not going to listen to you anymore, Herman. I'm beginning to see you very clearly now. You're a liar! A liar and a cross-dresser! And you exaggerate! Your poetry, *everything*! One great big exaggeration!"

"Well, I don't exaggerate your stupidity!" he shot back at her.

"You want to be a woman?" Cherry said. "Well, maybe I can change your mind!"

And she threw herself on him and ripped his wig off, then started ripping at his dress and trying to French kiss him. He was appalled, and said, "Get away, you dumb broad!"

They continued to struggle, roughing and tumbling on the bed. And he managed to reach out for his coin-heavy, pink plaster piggy bank, which was on the nightstand, and clouted Cherry on the head with it. He would not have done this if he had been himself, but this time she had strained his patience to the hilt. It was all her fault. Even though he was confused about his sexuality, he had enough maleness still in him to be chauvinistic at times, and like most men he was prone to blame everything on the woman in his life. He was sorry he had to knock Cherry unconscious. He had never thought of himself as a belligerent man – or woman. He was essentially nonviolent, and he felt shock and revulsion at this new revelation of the terrible forces locked inside his id.

He knew his relationship with Cherry was over, and he felt an uncontrollable urge to get out of the apartment. On the positive side, now that he was out of the closet he could wear his dresses anytime he wanted to, so he packed a few things and bugged out of there, sashaying down the street, wiggling his butt seductively in case anyone was watching, and thinking that he cut a fine figure in his feminine finery.

CHAPTER 35

Cherry, while she was unconscious, dreamed that she and Marcello Fettucini were together on a beach of white sand, somewhere in Italy, with snow-capped mountains in the distance and a tiny fishing village nearby making its presence felt but not seen. Marcello was kissing her and rubbing her body with olive oil, and she woke up calling his name out loud.

Unbeknownst to her, he was in jail. Not in a cell, but in an interrogation room. The cop who had arrested him, Sgt. Dooley, wanted to do him a favor by incarcerating him long enough to make him reconsider his notion of committing suicide. But the problem was that Marcello had been naked at the time of his arrest. This aroused the bloodhound instincts of Inspector Matt Sherlock, who ordered Marcello to be brought to him for intensive questioning. Dooley and a plainclothesman, Steve Blaze, were looking on while Sherlock pursued his line of reasoning.

"Next you're gonna tell me you were taking a piss!" the inspector bellered at Marcello. "I seen guys overdose before! You think I was born yesterday? Now don't tell me just because there ain't any tracks on your arm – where you shootin' the stuff, up your ass? You better come clean!"

He blew a cloud of cigar smoke into Marcello's face, a Marsh Wheeling, not half as strong as the De Nobilis Marcello was used to, so it didn't faze him. The De Nobilis looked like black ropes, and were just as harsh, and the smell of the Marsh Wheeling seemed like the breath of a baby by comparison.

"I think he's tellin' the truth," Steve Blaze chimed in, and he hitched up his shoulder holster because it was giving him an ulcer under his armpit.

Matt Sherlock shot Blaze an angry look for butting in and disrupting the line of questioning. Marcello flinched, under a new barrage of Sherlock's questions.

"How much you use a day?"

"Who's your connection?"

"Where do your stash your uncut stuff?"

"I think he's tellin' the truth," Blaze persisted. He knew he could sometimes influence Matt Sherlock just by sticking to his guns.

"Fettucini, I heard that name before," Sherlock mused

With a tingle of fear, it dawned on Marcello that the cops might have something on his brother, Angelo. "Pasta," he said, to distract them.

"Huh?" said Sherlock.

"Pasta," Blaze said, catching on. "Fettucini is pasta. That's where you musta heard the name before, boss."

Sherlock turned the deduction over in his mind.

"When I saw him on the bridge naked, he was just kneeling up there, mumbling to hisself," Dooley said.

"So how the hell was he gonna jump if he was *kneeling*?" Sherlock said. "That proves he wasn't gonna commit suicide. This oily dago is *lyin'* to us!"

"I was-a saying the Hail Mary," Marcello told the cops, in a weary, dejected tone. "I was-a gonna kill-a myself because life has-a become meaningless to me. I was-a a product tester inna a dildo factory, and since I no canna get a hard-on no more, I was-a gonna lose-a my job."

The cops burst out laughing, and it was a crushing, humiliating thing for Marcello to endure. Having arrived at the assumption that he was guilty, the cops had become callous about his personal feelings and unwilling to acknowledge his basic human dignity.

"You make a confession, maybe I'll go easy on ya," Matt Sherlock offered.

"Confession?" Marcello said. "You gonna call-a the priest for me? I canna go to confession, no?"

"*No!*" Sherlock said emphatically. "Take him back to his cell, Dooley. The rotten bastard disgusts me. I can't stand to look at him no more."

"We don't have nothin' to hold him on," Blaze pointed out. "No tracks on his arm. No junk. Nothing. We don't even have corroboration on the indecent exposure rap. No witnesses. We gotta let him go, boss."

"Goddamn it, it irks me!" Sherlock exploded. "We got him dead to rights, if we could find some evidence! Yet we gotta let the filthy scum walk the streets! The people are always screamin' for law and order but they won't give us the tools to do it with! Our fuckin' hands are *tied*!"

So, the next morning, after a lengthy but rather vague lecture from the judge, hitting all around what he had done and why he must never do it again, Marcello was given back his belt and his shoelaces and his necktie, and he was a free man again. Free, in Matt Sherlock's estimation, to perpetrate additional crimes against humanity, and he walked out of the precinct house into the sunlight and fresh air.

He stopped at the nearest phone booth, because for some reason Cherry Jankowski was filling his thoughts, and he had to get in touch with her. She was the only person in the whole world he wanted to talk to. He hesitated, then dropped his money in the slot and dialed. After several rings, there was a voice on the other end of the line.

"Good morning. Joyful Novelties."

"This is-a Marcello Fettucini."

"So?"

"Cherry Jankowski – may I please-a speak-a with her?"

"She hasn't come in to work today. No one knows where she is. Both of you are in big trouble. You're going to be *fired*."

Marcello slammed the phone down. He exited the phone booth and began to walk, aimlessly, with the air of a man in total despair, who does not know what his future holds.

CHAPTER 36

As Cherry gathered her wits about her, it surpised her that she had called out Marcello's name upon regaining consciousness – but after a while she remembered it clearly and there was no denying that she had done it. She still felt a little dizzy. But she could recall her dream vividly, especially the grand finale when she and Marcello were heatedly making love and --

The phone rang, interrupting her thoughts just when she was getting horny.

It rang again, but she did not move for it. When she finally did reach for it, it stopped ringing.

She got up slowly, staggered across the bedroom and looked at herself in the mirror. There was a bump on her head, very tender to the touch, but she brushed her hair forward to cover it, and this little cosmetic consideration cheered her a little.

She was in the mood to talk with someone – someone who would be warm and sympathetic and understanding enough to listen while she poured her heart out – so of course she thought of Thelma Bartholomew and grabbed the phone and dialed.

"Good morning. Joyful Novelties."

"Hello? Is Thelma there?"

"She left a while ago. Claimed she wasn't feeling well."

"Oh. I see."

"Anything I can help you with? We have a special on our XX20 Ultravibrator this week."

"No...no, thank you."

"I can switch you over to a salesman..."

As Cherry let the phone drop into its cradle, she was startled by a loud knock on her door. She caught her breath, thinking it was probably Herman. She went to answer it, as she tried to mentally prepare herself for a confrontation.

It turned out to be Thelma.

"Hi, honey," Thelma said, with a tentative smile.

"Thelma! I just tried to call you!" Cherry said. "I seem to have made a gigantic mess of *everything!"*

Just then there was another loud knock on the door, and unmindful of her nakedness, Cherry opened it. It was Stag the janitor, holding a packet of mail and a newspaper. "W-w-wow!" he stammered, his eyes bugged out at the sight of Cherry's voluptuous young naked body. "I - uh - h-h-here - your n-newsbody - er - p-p-p-paper."

"Thank you," Cherry said primly as she took her mail and the newspaper from him and tried half-heartedly to cover first her breasts then her public area with it.

"Who g-gave you the l-lump on your h-h-head?" Stag asked leeringly.

"Herman. Excuse me, I have to go, I have company."

"I b-b-bet you d-do," Stag said, knowingly. "H-h-herman prob'ly b-busted you in the h-head for g-g-goin' around showin' y-y-yer ass whenever h-he's not h-home."

Cherry slammed the door in his face, and once more he went to his room and made love to his artificial vagina while he dwelled on visions of Cherry heaving and thrusting beneath him, her long legs (which the truncated vagina did not have) wrapped around him, jerking and kicking at the moment of orgasm.

Cherry put on her nightgown, and she and Thelma sat on the sofa for a heart to heart talk. "I was worried about you," the older woman confided. "It's not like you not to show up for work. First Marcello disappears, then you. I thought something crazy might be going on. There's all kinds of nuts on the loose. Last year some lunatic was stabbing all the whores to death and cutting their tits off."

"No, nothing like that has happened to me," Cherry said. "Herman's gone, that's all."

"You're better off without him," Thelma pronounced.

"I know," Cherry admitted. "I guess I finally realized it. He wants to be a woman. Maybe he's going to have a sex change."

"To each his own," Thelma said.

"I wanted to think I was going to marry an intellectual," Cherry said. "As if it would rub off on me, or something. I know now that things don't come that easy. I've got to get my act together. I'm going to begin by resigning my position at Joyful."

"Atta girl! Hotdog! I knew you had it in ya!" Thelma exclaimed joyfully.

"I had a weird dream," Cherry confessed. "The most unlikely person appeared in it."

"Who?"

"Marcello," Cherry said softly, with a tremble she was unable to control. "I guess I might never see him again," she said wistfully.

"Buck up," said Thelma. "You know I love you like a daughter. I always want the best for you, honey. I'll say a Rosary for ya."

CHAPTER 37

Cherry felt terribly alone at the air terminal. She tried to pass the time by watching the planes come in. She had not bought her ticket yet, because she was not sure where she wanted to go.

Presumably the planes were full of people much more confident than she was, who knew where they had come from and where they wanted to be.

She left the observation area and walked down a long fluorescent corridor. She paused for a moment, not knowing where to go next – and suddenly she spotted Marcello! He was walking slowly, carrying a suitcase, and he looked unawares, as if walking in a dream.

"Marcello! Marcello!" she called out after him, and she hurried to catch up lest he turn a corner and vanish.

He stopped, dazed, when her voice finally penetrated his reverie. "Cherry I...but..." he stammered, at the sight of her and how beautiful she looked.

"Marcello! But...I thought...what are *you* doing here?"

Her heart fluttered when she looked at him.

"I'm-a leaving. Going back-a to Roma."

"But why?"

"I would-a rather die among-a the ruins. And-a you?"

"Oh, I don't know. Just watching the planes, I guess. The coming and the going. I guess I feel like the airport. Nothing's permanent. Herman left me. I'm a little mixed up. I might take a little vacation, to get my head together."

"You gotta a lump onna your head," he said.

"Herman conked me with his piggy-bank, the *brute*," Cherry said, and the idea of Herman being a brute made her laugh.

Marcello smiled and began walking, and because of his long strides Cherry had to hurry to keep up with him. "I had a dream about you," she said breathlessly, hoping he would stop and talk a while longer.

He did stop, and faced her, and once again her beauty made him a little nervous. "You hadda a dream? About *me*?"

"Yes, a wonderful dream. It was after Herman and I broke up."

"FLIGHT 715 NOW BOARDING FOR ROME."

The loudspeaker voice shattered their mood. "That's-a my flight," Marcello said, and he resumed walking hurriedly down the corridor toward the boarding area.

Once again Cherry found herself running after him. She was desperate to do something to stop him from leaving. She said, "Aren't you interested in my dream? In what you were *doing* in my dream?" she hinted shamelessly.

He stopped in his tracks, a puzzled look on his face. "What-a *could* I be doing?" he asked, giving a disparaging glance downward in the direction of his penis.

"You *were*," she told him, with a euphemistic wink and a smile.

"You mean? Inna the dream I was-a --" he stammered.

"Yes. *Yes!*" she told him.

"Capable of – inna your *dream?*"

"*Yes!*" she replied with growing excitement.

But he could not quite believe in her dream as a good omen, though he struggled to – and the loudspeaker blasted again, shattering his efforts.

"FLIGHT 715 NOW BOARDING FOR ROME."

"I'd-a better go. My plane," he said, with a glance at his wristwatch.

"Marcello, aren't you going to kiss me goodbye," Cherry said, with tears in her eyes, and somehow the tears made her even more beautiful. Marcello took her in his arms, and they kissed. It was a good, long kiss. And it was followed by another. And another. Soon they had their tongues in each other's mouths.

And Marcello, forgetting himself and where they happened to be – which was directly in front of the boarding area – reached inside Cherry's blouse and found that she was not wearing a bra, and he cupped her firm breasts in his hands and massaged her hardening nipples. And then – he began unfastening her blouse and taking it off, while she held him tightly and began squirming against him.

And people were beginning to stop and stare. They stared openly, glad to have something interesting to look at, to relieve the boredom of waiting for their flights to come in. Everyone was staring, even a priest who happened to be there waiting for a plane to take him to Rome to see the pope.

Oblivious to everything, Marcello and Cherry tumbled to the floor. He had his hands on her buttocks and on her crotch. And he began kissing her naked breasts and sucking her nipples.

Horrified, a gray-haired grandmother covered her nine-year-old grandson's eyes with the palms of her hands – while she herself continued to watch with considerable fascination, and she became moist in a certain place that had not responded that way in years, and she discovered at this late stage of her life that voyeurism turned her on but she resolved not to admit this to anyone.

Stimulated also, in spite of his best intentions, the priest knelt beside the sinning couple and began to pray, while the sinners continued to writhe and squirm and undress each other in what the priest considered a decadent display of public immorality, even though with this display before him he was having trouble keeping his mind on his duty and his calling. Fact is (I might as well tell it) the priest was getting an erection, and he was afraid that if he stopped kneeling and praying and stood up, people would see the bulge in his trousers.

It looked as though Marcello and Cherry were going to fornicate right there in the airline terminal, in the middle of the boarding area. Some of the onlookers were appalled, and some were curious, and some were utterly fascinated. One stern-looking fellow with a briefcase kept walking in circles around the half-nude couple and muttering what a disgrace it was and that somebody should throw some water on them. But he didn't make a move to get a bucket of water himself.

Nobody thought of calling a cop. It goes to show how people will go to pieces in an emergency.

Cherry groped for Marcello's crotch and began shouting joyfully, "It's up! It's up! Oh, thank god, Marcello – it's up!"

"Huh? What?" he said, getting to his feet and looking down at himself. And the look of joy that came over his face in that momentous moment would have melted the heart of a plaster statue! "Mama mia!" he exclaimed. And he made the Sign of the Cross and grabbed the still-kneeling priest and kissed him on both cheeks – just as the good Father was ejaculating in his trousers. But he thanked God that the bulge down there would go away now.

Cherry was already on her feet, buttoning her buttons and straightening her hair and trying in other hasty ways to make herself presentable. But she had already lost the respect of most of the people around her, even though a lot of them admired her body.

"Where we gonna go?" Marcello asked desperately, not wanting to lose what he had attained.

"My apartment!" Cherry blurted.

"Yes! Yes! Avanti!" Marcello shouted. "Hurry! These-a things are-a by no means guaranteed!"

They ran toward a parked taxi, Marcello crying, "It's up!" And the cab driver put his hands in the air, thinking it was a stickup – his third in as many weeks. "Take my money but don't shoot me," he said wearily. "I'll cooperate as usual. Nobody is more cooperative than I am." And he was glad he only had fifteen bucks on him this time.

"Oh, no, you don't understand," Cherry tried to explain. "He meant he was – his getting it – well, I mean—"

"Mama mia!" Marcello shouted, and he shoved them all into the cab and yelled, "Avanti! *Avanti!*" as they peeled out onto the highway after nearly careening into two other cars.

Cherry kept her hand on Marcello's crotch, safeguarding his accomplishment.

The cabbie appeared to be in a state of shock and ran several red lights on the way to Cherry's apartment. Marcello shoved two twenties in the guy's hand and did not wait for change. He ran up the stairs to the apartment, where Cherry already had her key in the lock.

They rushed into each other's arms in a mad embrace and began ripping at each other's clothes – and they did not notice Herman, who was sitting on the couch watching them, with a horrified expression on his face. He was still dressed as a woman, but in a new outfit that was frankly in poor taste. He had on an orange dress that was so long that it was out of fashion, and also a blue crocheted shawl that made him appear matronly, and a set of artificial pearls that were, in a word, outlandish. Hopefully, he would in time learn to dress more becomingly, maybe by subscribing to magazines like *Cosmopolitan*. His hair looked all right, the way he had it teased. But his rouge and lipstick were overdone. But his legs weren't bad, if a bit muscular.

By this time Cherry was totally nude, and Marcello was almost in the same condition.

"My god, Cherry!" Herman cried out in total indignation. "I know you're hung up on sex, but I never dreamed that your mind would become *this* diseased, just because I scorned you! Now you're bringing home *strangers*?"

Marcello's hard-won erection faltered. "Quista? Quista buffone?" he said angrily, as he went totally soft.

"A real nice how-do-you-do!" Herman ranted. "I'm gone less than forty hours and you're carrying on with another *person*!"

"Manage la mia!" Marcello said. "Quista this-a old lady? Cherry, is-a this-a your sister?"

"I was going to give it another try," Herman said. "I was going to lower myself to come back to you. I'm going to Sweden for a sex operation. But I thought we could still be roommates."

"Cherry – is-a this-a your sister?" Marcello repeated, and suddenly he realized (incorrectly) that Herman was Cherry's mother, and his face lit up and he felt he could become master of the situation. He had always had a way with mothers. "Aw, Mrs. Jankowski," he said soothingly. "I love-a your daughter. We gonna be married. I promise-a you, I no touch-a her till then."

"Beast! Get away from me!" Herman screamed, and he smacked Marcello with his purse.

"He's not my sister," Cherry mumbled. "And he's not my mother either."

She followed Herman to the doorway and stared after him as he clicked down the stairs a bit awkwardly in his high heels, but still he was doing so well that she realized he must've had plenty of practice. "Herman, don't go away mad," she called out to him.

"Call me Hermione from now on!" he yelled back. And he made his exit from Cherry's life.

Totally confused, Marcello wandered into the kitchen and found a bottle of bourbon, picked it up and guzzled.

At precisely this moment, Vernon Biggs popped out of his apartment and found Cherry nude in the hallway and totally defenseless, which is the way he liked her. "Wow!" he said. "Looky here!" And he couldn't believe his good luck.

"Get way from me, you sex maniac!" Cherry told him as she attempted to cover her public area with one hand and her right breast with the other and naturally she ran out of hands, which left the left breast exposed – and it was the one that Biggs grabbed.

He pressed Cherry against the wall and kissed her and tried to shove his five-inch penis straight into her. But that's when Marcello came to her rescue. He seized Biggs by his long hair, pulling some of it out by its roots, and spun Biggs around and administered a devastating uppercut that hit Biggs like a sledgehammer – and both Marcello and Cherry watched with considerable satisfaction as Biggs slid

141

down the wall and crumbled onto the floor with his five-inch erection still throbbing.

Cherry looked deeply into Marcello's eyes, her face radiating her love for him, along with her pride and admiration for the manly deed he had just performed. And Marcello looked at Cherry's beauty and voluptuousness, which he felt he richly deserved now that he had proven his manhood in physical combat. Although these kinds of feelings had gone somewhat out of fashion, the reality of them could not be denied, and they were sweet and wonderful feelings for a man and woman to experience.

Cherry and Marcello fell into each other's arms again and were soon both bare naked. He attained a throbbingly solid erection. And they kissed over the unconscious body of the vanquished Biggs, who unknown to them was being tormented by a nightmare filled with Welch's grape juice bottles.

And Stag the janitor came up from the basement to find out the cause of the racket, and caught a glimpse of Cherry's luscious buttocks just as she and Marcello ducked back into her apartment and closed the door. Stag glanced momentarily at Biggs and snickered when he saw how small Biggs' penis was, and then he went back down to his room and crawled back into bed with his artificial vagina.

As for Cherry and Marcello, they found themselves undeniably in love. And his magnificent 7.73 inch penis was ramming and prodding inside her. And the orgasm they both reached was simultaneous and felt like bombs going off and the earth opening up and bells ringing and the stars falling from the skies. And her nipples were erect afterwards and she had a slight rash on her chest, which according to sex experts is the unmistakable sign of orgasm in the human female.

In the summer after their marriage, they visited Italy. Marcello's brother Angelo came over for a few days and spent a lot of time walking in the hills with two swarthy Italians who always carried long-barreled shotguns, and then somebody's car blew up and Angelo left suddenly one day and the rumor circulated that the explosion had inadvertently killed somebody's wife.

Nevertheless, Cherry and Marcello were blissfully on their own again, and they stayed for two weeks in a quaint fishing village on the Mediterranean, and they made love on the sand and rubbed each other all over with olive oil, thus fulfilling Cherry's dream, which was the dream that had brought them together and had prevented him from going back to Italy all alone.

"I'm so happy," she said. "So *happy!*" she repeated, as she nestled against him in the sun.

"It's-a because we quitta our jobs," he said, and he breathed a kiss into her ear, and she knew they would make love again back in their hotel room.

She touched his cheek lightly and looked lovingly at his sunburned Roman nose with its skin peeling and hanging down in flakes. "You really think it's because we quit our jobs?" she asked him, because all her questions were directed at him now, and Herman was a thing of the past, even though he had sent them a postcard from Sweden.

"The dildo factory is-a *plastic*." Marcello said. "No good for you and-a me. We are *real-a* people. We no canna live inna plastic."

She reached inside his bathing trunks and took his penis in her hand, and it immediately began to harden. And the sun shined down on them and on all of Italy.

And they lived happily ever after, except for a few minor setbacks.

ABOUT THE AUTHOR

With twenty books published internationally and nineteen feature movies in worldwide distribution, John Russo has been called a "living legend." He began by co-authoring the screenplay for NIGHT OF THE LIVING DEAD, which has become recognized as a "horror classic." His three books on the art and craft of movie making have become bibles of independent production, and one of them, SCARE TACTICS, won a national award for Superior Nonfiction. Quentin Tarantino and many other noted filmmakers have stated that Russo's books helped them launch their careers.

John Russo wants people to know he's "just a nice guy who likes to scare people" – and he's done it with novels and films such as RETURN OF THE LIVING DEAD, MIDNIGHT, THE MAJORETTES, THE AWAKENING and HEARTSTOPPER. He has had a long, rewarding career, and he shows no signs of slowing down. Recently his screenplay for ESCAPE OF THE LIVING DEAD was made into a five-part comic book released by Avatar to great acclaim; it made the Top Ten of Horror Comics nationally and spawned two graphic novels and ten sequels.

Russo's recent novel is THE HUNGRY DEAD, was published by Kensington Books. He is also slated to direct two movies: a remake of his cult hit, MIDNIGHT, and a brand new take on the "zombie phenomenon" entitled SPAWN OF THE DEAD.

Russo's latest novels DEALEY PLAZA, THE ACADEMY, THE AWAKENING, THE BOOBY HATCH and LIVING THINGS are published by Burning Bulb Publishing. His short story CHANNEL 666 appears in THE BIG BOOK OF BIZARRO.

His popularity among genre fans remains at a high pitch. He appears at many movie conventions each year as a featured guest, and he considers his appearance at the Orion Festival, hosted by Kirk Hammett and METALLICA, one of the highlights of his career.

For more information on John Russo,
his books, movies, or official merchandise,
please visit:

www.TheJohnRusso.com

You've just read the book, now watch the movie!

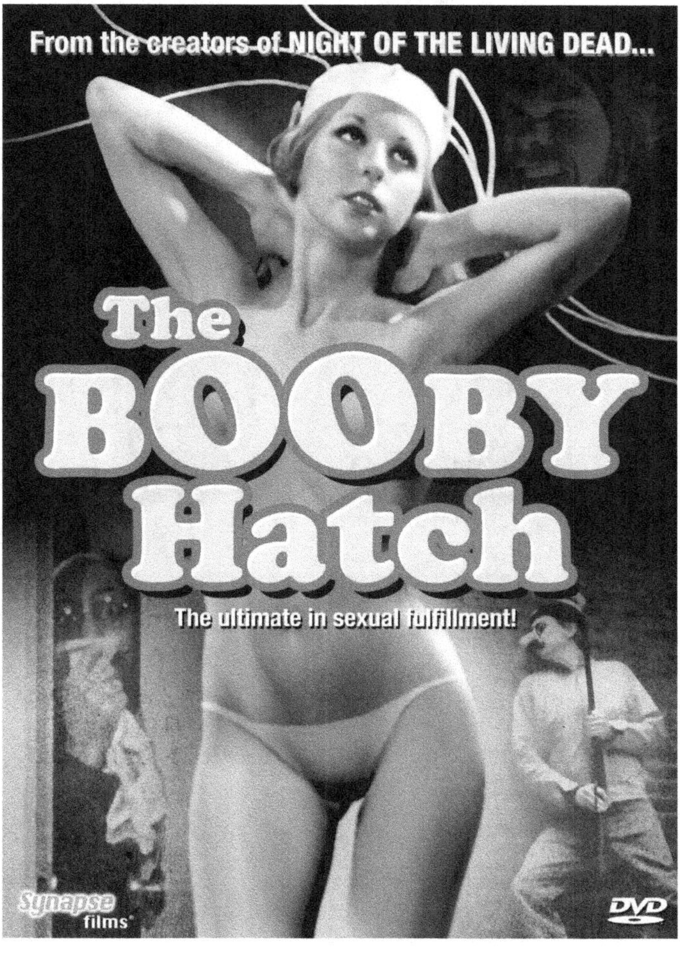

Available on DVD at

www.TheJohnRusso.com
www.BurningBulbPublishing.com

Burning Bulb
PUBLISHING

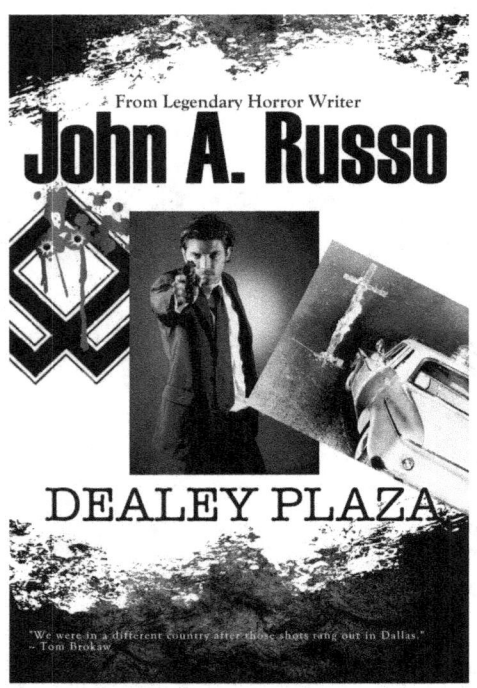

DEALEY PLAZA

From legendary horror and suspense writer JOHN RUSSO comes a harrowing tale where no one is safe!

Dealey Plaza is one of the most notorious places in America, and when youthful conspiracy buffs go there in 1964 to stage their own reenactment of the Kennedy Assassination, four of them are brutally murdered ~ the first victims of a hate-filled legacy that continues for four more decades.

The survivors of that long-ago Dallas trip, each of them now icons of the American way of life, are about to be honored ~ or killed.

Who will live and who will die? Will it be country-western star Lori McCoy? Her loving husband? Her scheming ex-husband? Or the case-hardened FBI agent and longtime friend who risks his life trying to protect them?

www.DealeyPlazaBook.com

Burning Bulb
PUBLISHING

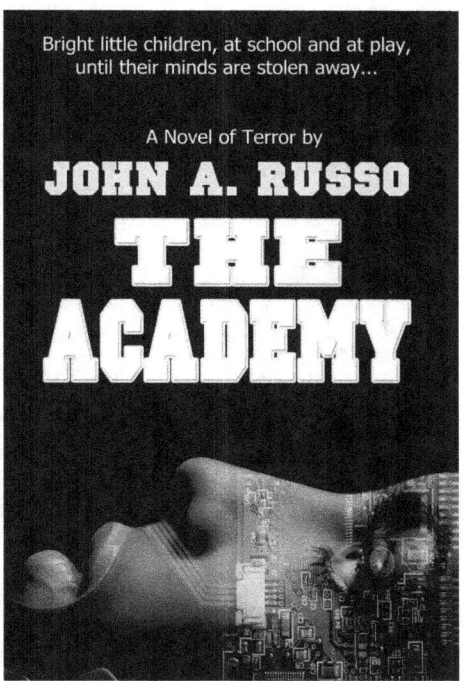

Bright little children, at school and at play,
until their minds are stolen away...

A Novel of Terror by

JOHN A. RUSSO

THE ACADEMY

THE ACADEMY

The Academy. It's every parent's dream, turning their little darlings into geniuses, superachievers, perfect little children.

And if there's a problem, the Academy fixes that too. It's a simple operation. Just a little device. Then a teeny pink scar on a tender little skull . . .

One boy knows the secret. Now he wants his mind back. But it's much, much too late. Too late for anything but the ugly feelings. The bad feelings. The messy sexy feelings. The knife-cold hatred, the murderous rage, for total, screaming, blood-drenching revenge . . .

www.TheJohnRusso.com

Burning Bulb
PUBLISHING

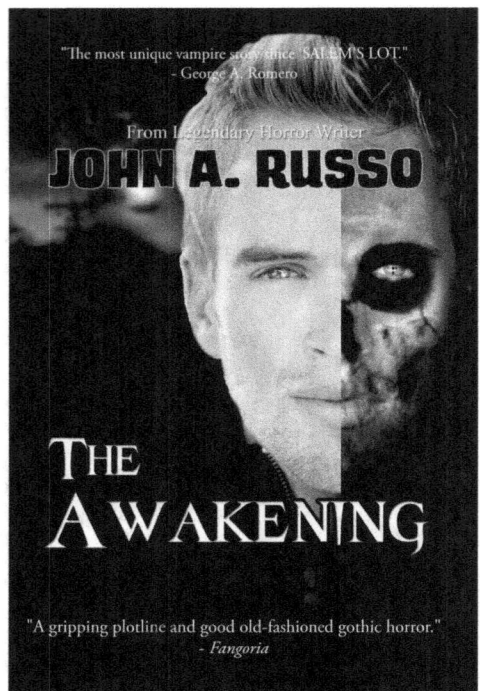

THE AWAKENING

For two hundred years, he has rested. Now he rises. Now he will be satisfied. Nothing can stop him. No one can resist him.

Benjamin Latham is young and handsome, his eighteenth-century mind wakened to a bizarre twentieth-century world. And there is the need deep within . . . an animal need, frightening, murderous, unholy . . . a vital need that must be fed.

And with his need comes a power over men and women to do his bidding, to quiet his dark craving . . .

Until the murders begin. And the inquiries. All suggesting the same hideous truth.

Now Benjamin must find a sanctuary: a lover, a partner, a friend. Someone who can share his darkness. Someone he can lead to . . . The Awakening.

www.TheJohnRusso.com

Burning Bulb
PUBLISHING

"A sense of infectious fun, straight from the author's pen."
— Nightmare Library

From Legendary Horror Writer
JOHN A. RUSSO

LIVING THINGS

"Russo carries his talent for the horrific neatly over into the novel form."
— West Coast Review of Books

LIVING THINGS

Beneath the shimmering Miami sun sprawls one of the Mafia's biggest empires, a glittering world of lavish beachfront mansions, neon-painted nightclubs, beautiful women, expensive cars—and absolute control over the state's billion-dollar drug trade. But, one by one, its ganglords and henchmen are falling prey to a new rival. His powers are fueled by monstrous ancient rituals; his hellish undead legions slaughter mobsters and innocent citizens alike, his unholy lust for power is virtually unstoppable.

Now a burned-out ex-detective and a brilliant anthropologist must enter a gruesome, nightmare world to fight this master of malevolence and illusion. Their time is short, their weapons few, and they face an ultimate, terrifying choice - annihilation or the loss of their souls to the eternal torment of those who never die. . .

www.TheJohnRusso.com

Burning Bulb
PUBLISHING

NIGHT OF THE LIVING DEAD

Why does **Night of the Living Dead** hit with such chilling impact?
Is it because everyday people in a commonplace house are suddenly the
victims of a monstrous invasion? Or is it because the ghouls who surround
the house with grasping claws were once ordinary people, too?

Decide for yourself as you read, and the horror grips you. All the
cannibalism, suspense and frenzy of the smash-hit move are here in the
novel.

www.TheJohnRusso.com

Burning Bulb
PUBLISHING

OTHER GREAT TITLES FROM

Burning Bulb

PUBLISHING

WWW.BURNINGBULBPUBLISHING.COM

ANTHOLOGIES
BIZARRO AND TRANSGRESSIVE FICTION

THE BIG BOOK OF BIZARRO

The Big Book of Bizarro brings together the peculiar prose of an international cast of the most grotesquely-gonzo, genre-grinding modern writers who ever put pen to paper (or mouse to pad), including:

NIGHT OF THE LIVING DEAD horror writers John Russo & George Kosana; HUSTLER MAGAZINE erotica contributors Eva Hore, Andrée Lachapelle, & J. Troy Seate and established Bizarro genre authors D. Harlan Wilson, William Pauley III, Wol·vriey, Laird Long, Richard Godwin and so many more!

From Alien abductions to Zombie sex, The Big Book of Bizarro contains OVER FIFTY STORIES of the most outrélandish transgressive fiction that you'll ever lay your capricious and curious hands upon!

WARNING: This book may be one of the most controversial and dangerous books you'll ever read.

WESTWARD HOES

Nine outlaw writers rode into town from obscurity to pen nine tantalizing tales of horror and fantasy, and leaving once they branded their own personal marks on the weird western genre and became living legends of the American Frontier experience.

Like drunken Indian scouts, the writers fervidly tracked down and captured the Western genre, tore off its fashionable veneer and ravished its exposed essence.

So belly up to the bar with your favorite soiled dove and enjoy perusing these thrilling tales of Old West debauchery, danger and desire; compiled by the publisher of The Big Book of Bizarro and featuring the bizarro novella *Big Trouble in Little Ass* by Wol-vriey.

ANTHOLOGIES
BIZARRO AND TRANSGRESSIVE FICTION

THE BIG BOOK OF BIZARRO SPECIAL KINDLE EDITIONS

OTHER AWESOME COLLECTIONS

GARY LEE VINCENT'S
DARKENED
THE WEST VIRGINIA VAMPIRE SERIES

DARKENED HILLS

When evil descends on a small West Virginia town, who will survive?

Jonathan did not start out his life to become a rambler, it just worked out that way. William was a troubled youth with something to hide. Both were from Melas, a small town tucked away in the West Virginia hills... a town where disappearances are happening more and more frequently.

After the suicide of a wanted serial killer, the townsfolk thought the nightmare was over. But when a centuries-old vampire is discovered they find out the hard way it's just getting started. Dark secrets can only stay hidden for so long and when the devil comes to collect, there will be hell to pay. Can Jonathan and William find a way to stop the vampire before it's too late? Find out in *Darkened Hills!*

DARKENED HOLLOWS

In the heart-stopping sequel to the award-winning *Darkened Hills*, Jonathan and William must return to West Virginia to face possible criminal charges stemming from their last visit to the damned town of Melas, where both had narrowly escaped the clutches of a vampire seethe.

And as livestock start mysteriously getting murdered with all of their blood drained, worried farmers are searching for answers - leaving the local Sheriff and his deputy racing against time to learn the cause before a more violent crime is committed.

Burning Bulb
PUBLISHING

WWW.DARKENEDHILLS.COM

GARY LEE VINCENT'S
DARKENED
THE WEST VIRGINIA VAMPIRE SERIES

DARKENED WATERS

When the world goes to hell, the chosen must arise!

As Talman Cane orchestrates a flood of epic proportions in this third installment of the *Darkened* series the towns of Melas and Tarklin are caught completely off guard by the deluge. Hell-bent on finishing what they started, the evil brothers return to the lunatic asylum to take care of the witnesses and add to the ever-growing army of the undead.

Aided by Lucifer himself and the insane vampire demon Legion, the stage is set to channel all of the forces of hell to come forth. In an all-out race to survive, Jonathan, William, and Amanda soon discover they are up against impossible odds as Lucifer opens the Gateway to Hell, ushering in the zombie apocalypse and the End Times.

DARKENED SOULS

Melas and the Madison House are about to be rebuilt.
True evil is about to be reborne!

Young ex-priest and vampire-killer William is drawn back to the West Virginian town that almost killed him, where his vampire arch-enemy Victor Rothenstein still stalks the earth.

The town of Melas lies destroyed after the battle of the End of Days. But why is wealthy Jackie Nixon so eager to rebuild it using the bone dust of murdered souls?

Terrible evil has visited before, but the Gateway to Hell is about to be reopened in a horrific climax. And this time – it's personal.

WWW.DARKENEDHILLS.COM

Burning Bulb
PUBLISHING

WEST VIRGINIA-THEMED HUMORROROTICA

BY RICH BOTTLES JR.

HELLHOLE WEST VIRGINIA

From the heights of Mothman's perch high atop the Silver Bridge in Point Pleasant to the depths of Hellhole Cavern in Pendleton County, evil lurks within the shadows as the sun sets upon the haunted hills and hollows of West Virginia.

Bizarro author Rich Bottles Jr. blows the coffin lid off horror genre clichés with this tour de force cast of Eco-friendly vampires, beach-yearning zombies and sex-starved she-devils.

LUMBERJACKED

If you are easily offended or do not possess a truly depraved sense of humor, this story may not be the light summer reading fare you desire. As for the four feisty female freshmen stranded on top of West Virginia's third highest mountain, they have no choice but to experience the sick, twisted debauchery and perverted mayhem described deep inside the tight unbroken bindings of this horrific missive.

Lumberjacked takes the reader to a nightmarish world where character development and aesthetic integrity are prematurely cut short by the swinging axes of maniacal lumberjacks, who are hell bent on death and destruction in the remote forests of Appalachia. And at the climax, when paranoia crosses over to the paranormal, Lumberjacked makes Deliverance look like a family raft trip down the Lower Gauley.

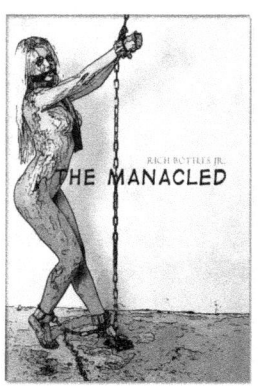

THE MANACLED

What happens when twin brothers lease out the former West Virginia State Penitentiary with the false purpose of filming a documentary on supernatural phenomena, but their true intention is to make a pornographic movie?

Chaos ensues as the disturbed spirits of murdered convicts, along with the reanimated dead from the neighboring Indian Burial Mound, take their vengeance on the unwary and undressed trespassers.

Zombies, ghosts, mobsters and porn collide in this bizarro tale from horror author Rich Bottles Jr.

Burning Bulb
PUBLISHING

WOL-VRIEY
BIZARRO AND TRANSGRESSIVE FICTION

Burning Bulb
PUBLISHING

BOSTON POSH

In 2028 AD, the USA is a nation ravaged by hungry dragons and dinosaurs. In Boston, Massachusetts, private eye Bud Malone is hired to rescue a kidnapped heiress. But nothing is as it seems. Malone works to unravel a tangled web involving Boston Chinatown, a 200-year-old woman with a 9-year-old body, white robots, a human-liver-eating psychopath, a golem, a porcelain dragon, and a snake goddess with a crush on him. There's also a woman obsessed with chicken sex. Then Malone meets Posh Lane, a gorgeous call girl who's desperate to quit her pimp. Romantic sparks ignite between Posh and Malone, but Posh's past suddenly catches up with her in a BIG way. To save Posh, Malone agrees to run a quest for Earth's new rulers, the Forks. But, Malone has no idea that agreeing to the Fork's odd request will send him on the weirdest trip he's ever been on in his life.

VEGAN VAMPIRE VAGINAS

The biggest bank heist in US history. And Tom Palmer can't remember pulling it off. And no, this isn't your standard case of amnesia. After a one-night-stand gone horribly wrong, Boston salesman Tom Palmer wakes up with a vagina implanted in his left hand. Then his day gets worse:

Tom is transported across space-time to a nightmare version of Boston, one where the Bizarro virus has transformed half the population into cannibals. Worst of all, Tom discovers that in this new Boston, he's the infamous gangster Pussypalm, wanted for robbing the Federal Reserve Bank of Boston a year ago. He also learns that the vagina in his hand is prophetic, i.e. it talks . . . after sex. With 130 people left dead during his bank heist and six billion dollars missing, Tom knows he's living on borrowed time. It is in his best interests not to remember anything. Because once he does . . .

VEGAN ZOMBIE APOCALYPSE

In the post-apocalypse worlderness, zombies rule the earth. They're allergic to meat, and brains literally make them explode. Zombies now eat blood potatoes, parasitic tubers grown in the flesh of humancows corralled in maximum security farms. Two fugitives meet in the ancient ruins of Texas. The first is Soil 15-f, a womancow who's escaped her farm a week before she's due to be killed and her blood potato crop harvested. The second fugitive is Able Kane, former head necros food technician, now sentenced to death for heresy. But Soil is no ordinary humancow. Unknown to herself, she's the vegan zombie agricultural revolution, and the zombies desperately want her back. And the necros equally desperately want Able Kane dead. He's fled with a forbidden discovery which will reshape the world for the worse if used. And Able is just hardheaded/misguided enough to use it.

MINOR CONFESSIONS OF AN ANGEL FALLING UPWARD

by Planner Forthright, as edited by Joey Madia

Confession. Revelation. Rant. *Minor Confessions of an Angel Falling Upward* is all of these... and more. Set in modern times and spiraling back to the swirl of Pre-Creation, this postmodern blend of genre-bending pop-prose and socio-political commentary is a classic tale of the (anti-)hero's quest for Reason and Redemption in a Universe gone mad.

Who is Planner Forthright? A fallen angel made Man. A once-winged evil with un-Divine purpose on this Plane. A cannibal prince chosen to inherit a castled landscape of destruction and despair. An Alchemist of sorts—a mental magician; a mortar-and-pestle wizard converting carbon lies to golden Truth, whose language is his own. A Vampire by nature and condition whose been walking the waters and thorny highways of our planet for over 40 years. And he's seeking a way out...

PASSAGEWAY

by Gary Lee Vincent with illustrations by Andy Hopp

When an archeological dig goes horribly wrong, the team is trapped in an alternate world where evil awaits them at every turn. Find out who will survive the *Passageway*!

From Gary Lee Vincent, the author of supernatural vampire thriller *Darkened Hills*, comes an unforgettable tale that spans four continents and takes the reader to the very realm of Hell itself.

Skeleton warriors, zombies, other undead beings and werewolves are allvery real inside the *Passageway*! In this Bizarro-genre tribute to H.P. Lovecraft and Indiana Jones, this deadly tale will keep you guessing and leave you breathless to the end!

THE TWELVE STEPS

by Zachary Crabtree

"A Man who Cannot Keep Awake Cannot Keep it Together." There is always something that pulls an alcoholic deeper into his unquenchable thirst – something degenerative to the human spirit. Indeed, there have been incidents in my life that carry tragic significance to me, yet I know they pale in comparison to the tragedies experienced by others.

When the jagged pieces of a disfigured past become a troubled, broken-up, glass-bottled mosaic in one's present life, all the innocent souls affected along the way become entangled in one's conscience; while the depression, pills, manic behavior and soul-searching coalesce in a series of twelve steps.

Alcohol affects the lives of hooligans, stubborn old fools, lovers, and families torn apart by drunk drivers – drunk drivers like me.

Burning Bulb
PUBLISHING

THE FALL OF TOMORROW

Hopelessness... How do you protect your loved ones when Hell itself opens its insidious mouth?
Horror... Nightmarish Creatures invade your world and there is nowhere to hide.
Blood... How long can you hold out before they come for you?
Pain... Where do you run to avoid being eaten alive by monsters with a voracious appetite for your flesh?
Screams... While you selfishly run for your own life.
Questions... Who is to blame? Where did they come from? How many people survived...and how does the human race find the means to fight back?

THE FALL OF TOMORROW is man's last tale of desperation told by those that are striving to salvage some hope against a ravenous bastion of evil beasts bent on ruling our world.

"David Fairhead writes compelling stories that offer very human characters and very inhuman monsters. There is no subtlety in Fairhead's imagination - he is simply dying to scare the hell out of you."
- Nelson W Pyles - author of DEMONS, DOLLS AND MILKSHAKES

Burning Bulb
PUBLISHING

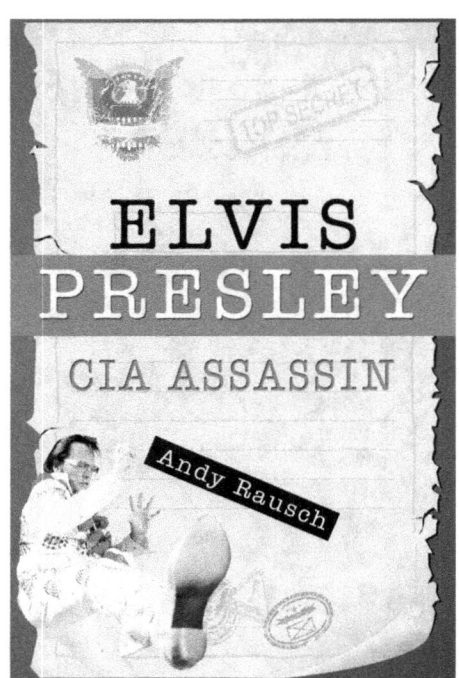

ELVIS PRESLEY, CIA ASSASSIN

"I can guarantee you. Read this book and you'll never look at Elvis the same way again!"
~ Douglas Brode, author of ELVIS CINEMA AND POPULAR CULTURE

SOON TO BE A MAJOR MOTION PICTURE

In 1970, singer Elvis Presley secretly met with President Richard Nixon. This new comedic novel imagines that Presley became a Central Intelligence Agency operative, eventually moving up through the ranks to become a skilled assassin.

Presented in an oral history fashion, the book tells us about Presley's secret transformation by the people who knew him best.

Did he fake his death in 1977? Was Presley involved with the Watergate scandal? The Iran hostage crisis? Communicating with aliens?

Read this book to find out the answers to these and many more questions.

Burning Bulb
PUBLISHING